"It's kind of interesting to look at who we were then and where we are now. Life has a way of changing us."

"Isn't that the truth?" She'd gone pensive on him, gaze somewhere in the distance.

"Aw, come on. You weren't so bad."

"You always were the nicest guy. With an apparently faulty memory." She motioned toward the paper in his hand. "So what do you think? Any ideas for me?"

She was shutting off the conversation, unwilling to talk about herself anymore, but for a moment he'd glimpsed the young girl she used to be. He'd seen some things in her expression that surprised him. Hurt. Regret. Sadness.

Troubled, he turned his attention to the list, though he was more aware of Lana Ross than he wanted to be.

He swallowed, bothered to be thinking about her, not as a neighbor in need as he'd told his sister, but as a beautiful, interesting woman an arm's length away.

Books by Linda Goodnight

LINDA GOODNIGHT

Winner of a RITA® Award for excellence in inspirational fiction, Linda Goodnight has also won a Booksellers' Best Award, an ACFW Book of the Year award and a Reviewers' Choice Award from *RT Book Reviews*. Linda has appeared on the Christian bestseller list and her romance novels have been translated into more than a dozen languages. Active in orphan ministry, this former nurse and teacher enjoys writing fiction that carries a message of hope and light in a sometimes dark world. She and her husband live in Oklahoma. Visit her website at www.lindagoodnight.com. To browse a current listing of Linda Goodnight's titles, please visit www.Harlequin.com.

Sugarplum
Homecoming

Linda Goodnight

HARLEQUIN® LOVE INSPIRED®

Recycling programs
for this product may
not exist in your area.

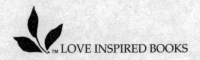

™ LOVE INSPIRED BOOKS

ISBN-13: 978-0-373-81733-7

SUGARPLUM HOMECOMING

Copyright © 2013 by Linda Goodnight

All rights reserved. Except for use in any review, the reproduction
or utilization of this work in whole or in part in any form by any
electronic, mechanical or other means, now known or hereafter
invented, including xerography, photocopying and recording, or in
any information storage or retrieval system, is forbidden without
the written permission of the editorial office, Love Inspired Books,
233 Broadway, New York, NY 10279 U.S.A.

This is a work of fiction. Names, characters, places and incidents are
either the product of the author's imagination or are used fictitiously, and
any resemblance to actual persons, living or dead, business establishments,
events or locales is entirely coincidental.

This edition published by arrangement with Love Inspired Books.

® and TM are trademarks of Love Inspired Books, used under license.
Trademarks indicated with ® are registered in the United States Patent
and Trademark Office, the Canadian Trade Marks Office and in other
countries.

www.Harlequin.com

Printed in U.S.A.

Let he who is without sin cast the first stone.
—*John* 8:7

Prologue

"Come *on,* Nathan," nine-year-old Paige whispered with urgency. "Hurry before Daddy wakes up."

Nathan cast a worried eye toward his father sprawled on a blanket beneath a tree, hands behind his head. The remnants of an early autumn picnic were strewn about the quiet glade deep in the Ozark Mountains. "We're going to get in trouble."

Paige fisted a hand on one slight hip. "Do you want a mom or not?"

Nathan's gray gaze went from his dad to the twenty-foot-high waterfall only yards away. "Well, yeah, but Whisper Falls is kind of big and scary."

Impatiently, Paige tugged on her little brother's arm. He could be such a baby sometimes. "You can do it, brother. God will help you."

Paige knew her brother well. Give him a challenge, tell him God was in it, and he would give everything he had. Which wasn't much considering how little he was.

As she expected, Nathan thrust out his dinosaur T-shirt and trotted toward the waterfall. The noise from the water tumbling over the mountainside *was* really loud but not that scary to Paige. Daddy had brought them here before. They loved Whisper Falls. They loved wading in the pool below, beyond the foam and current, where even now three teenagers splashed and yelled.

But fun wasn't Paige's mission today. She'd thought up the picnic as an excuse to get here, to do the one thing she was certain would bring her their heart's desire. To pray. Everybody said it was true. The story was in the brochures all over town. Anyone brave enough to reach the secret place behind the falls would get their prayer answered. And Paige had decided the time was now.

With her pointed chin as determined as her brother's, Paige jogged toward Whisper Falls. Nathan tagged along, a little reluctant but willing. Like her, he was ready to do anything to get a mom.

They reached the slippery gray rock face and started the climb. Natural cleaves in the mountainside offered a foothold but over the years so many people had made the climb that the path was well worn. If they clung tight, like the slugs Joel Snider brought to fourth grade for show-and-tell, they'd make it all the way up to God's special place.

"Why do we have to pray up *here?*" Nathan

asked, his face wrinkled with worry as he crept along in front of her, small hands gripping the rocks. If Daddy caught them, they'd have to do more than pray to get out of trouble.

Paige grunted as she took another handhold and waited for her brother to inch forward. The waterfall grew louder by the second, so she raised her voice. "I told you already. We're on a mission. Like in the movies when that guy had to bring back the ring to save the world. We have to prove ourselves worthy of a new mom."

"Oh."

She hoped that satisfied him for now because she was getting out of breath trying to talk and climb. Climbing was harder than she'd imagined. Harder than the sixth graders said. Maybe none of them had really climbed the falls at all.

"We're almost there," she huffed.

Paige glanced down and wished she hadn't. Daddy looked tiny, like a Ken doll, and the pool looked huge and bubbly. Spray dampened her skin. The smells of trees and leaves and water swirled like the pool below. One of the teenagers saw her and pointed.

Please, please, don't let him tell.

She gave a casual nod, hoping the teen believed she wasn't nearly as scared as she was. When she turned back toward the climb, Nathan was gone!

Panic seized her. Her hands were cold and wet, but she climbed faster, praying that the stories were true, that a secret room existed behind the water-fall, that Nathan hadn't fallen to his death.

She stretched her leg as far as her muscles would go, felt a foothold with the toe of her tennis shoe and lunged…and found herself standing on a wide ledge behind a terrifying rush of water. There was Nathan grinning at her.

"This is way cool."

Paige heaved a shaky sigh. "Let's pray and get out of here fast."

"I like it up here." He stuck his fingers into the violent spray of water *whooshing* in front of them.

Paige grabbed his hand and pushed him back. She had to get him out of here before he did some-thing childish. Like fall off the mountain. "Never mind about that. Close your eyes and think about Jesus and a new mom."

"But—"

"Do it, Nathan. Dad might wake up any minute."

This was enough to get his attention. He nodded and clasped his hands beneath his chin. "Okay. Do we want a mom with blond hair or brown hair?"

"Silly, I don't care about that kind of stuff. I want a mom who reads to us and tucks us in and bakes cupcakes for school parties."

"Daddy does that. Well, except for the cupcakes. He gets those at the bakery."

"That's not the point. We need a mom. Dad can't even fix my hair." She slapped at the side of her super short cut, the only kind of hairstyle Daddy could manage. She was nearly ten, for goodness' sake. Most of all she longed for a mother to love. Sometimes her heart hurt so bad at night when she prayed that she thought it might burst right out of her chest.

"I want a mom with brown hair," Nathan said stubbornly. "Our other mom had brown hair."

Paige smothered a sigh. She loved her brother a great big lot but sometimes he didn't understand what was really important. Not the way she did. "Then pray for a mom with brown hair. I don't care. Just pray."

With all the reverence she'd been taught in Sunday school and children's church since the day she was born, Paige folded her hands beneath her chin.

"Dear God, we need a mom. Daddy needs a wife. He's been sad long enough and Aunt Jenny says it's time for him to move on. Please send us a mother. Before Christmas would be nice."

"With brown hair."

Paige opened one eye. Nathan didn't even remember their mother. He'd only seen pictures. Like the one at Daddy's bedside. A piece of her heart felt really sad for him about that. "Yes, God, if it's not too much to ask, send a great mom with brown hair. And make her pretty so Daddy will like her, too. Amen."

"Amen."

"Now, let's get out of here before Daddy wakes up."

"How do we get down?"

Oh, boy, she'd not considered that part.

"Nathan! Paige! Where are you?" Daddy's voice came as a faint but worried echo through the silver curtain of water.

Nathan turned accusing eyes on his sister. "We are in so much trouble."

Chapter One

Bad pennies always return. But what about bad people?

Lana Ross stepped up on the wooden porch of the weathered old two-story house. Her heart hammered painfully against her ribs. She'd not wanted to come to this place of bad memories. She'd had to.

A stern inner voice, the voice of hard-won peace, moved her forward, toward the door, toward the interior. A house couldn't hurt her. If she'd been alone perhaps she would have given in to the shaky knees and returned to the car. But she wasn't alone.

Lana aimed a wink at the child at her side. Sydney was her everything now and no memories were allowed to keep this nine-year-old darling from having her very first permanent home.

"Is this where you lived when you were my age?" Sydney asked, her vivid turquoise eyes alive with interest.

"Uh-huh, Tess and I grew up here." Grew up. Yanked up. Kicked out.

A tangle of a vanilla-scented vine, overgrown and climbing upon the porch and around the paint-peeled pillar at one end, gave off a powerfully sweet smell. She didn't remember the bush being there before, especially this late in the fall. But then, she'd not seen this place in thirteen years. Not since she was eighteen and free to leave without looking over her shoulder for the long arm of the law.

With the sour taste of yesterday in her throat, Lana inserted the tarnished key into the front door, an old-time lock a person could peer through, and after a few tries felt the tumbler click. Breath held, she pushed the door open on its creaky hinges, but didn't step inside. Not yet. She needed a minute to be certain the house was empty, though she had the death certificate in her bag. Mama was dead. Had been for a couple of years. As far as she knew her entire family was dead. All except Lana and Tess and precious Sydney.

She couldn't make herself go inside. Everything was still and quiet in the dim living room, but inside her head Lana heard the yells, the fights, the horrible names she'd believed and mostly earned.

She and her twin sister, Tess, were no more and no less than what their mother had made them. Now, all these years later, Lana was determined to be more for Sydney's sake.

"We'll be happy here," Sydney declared with childlike confidence.

"Yes, we will." *If I have to fight the universe, you will have what you need and you will never, ever again live on the streets or inside a broken-down car.*

"Can we go in now? I want to see my room. You said I could have my own room, remember? And we'd fix it up fit for a princess? Remember?"

"I remember." The child's enthusiasm stirred Lana to action. Sydney had never had a room of her own. She'd never had a house. They'd lived here and there, in tiny one-room apartments and cheap hotels, all in pursuit of Lana's impossible dream. Most important of all, Sydney would be safe here. No one would ever expect Lana to return to the one place she'd tried so hard to escape. Especially Sydney's mother.

"Who's that?" Sydney asked from her spot half in and half out of what had once been the front parlor.

Across the street a man and two children stood in a neatly mowed yard watching them. Lana's stomach dropped into her resoled cowboy boots. It couldn't be. Surely not.

The thought had no more than crossed her mind than the sandy-brown haired man with the all-American good looks lifted a hand to wave and then started toward them. Two young children, close to Sydney's age, skipped along as if on an adventure.

Lana froze, one hand on the doorknob and the

other gripping Sydney's as if Davis Turner would snatch her up and carry her away.

"Hello," he said when he reached the end of the cracked sidewalk leading to the two-story.

Yep. He was Davis Turner all right. Mr. Clean-cut and Righteous. He'd been a year ahead of her in school. No one in Whisper Falls had a smile as wide, as easy and as bright as Davis.

Please God, don't let him recognize me.

"Hi," she said, not bothering to smile.

"You moving into the old Ross place?" Davis slipped his hands into the back pocket of his jeans, relaxed and easy in his skin. The man was much like the boy she remembered.

"We are."

"Great." He flashed that smile again. White straight teeth, easy, flexible skin that had weathered nicely, leaving happy spokes around grayish-blue eyes and along his cheeks. "The house has been empty a long time. Houses need people to keep them young and healthy."

What an interesting thing to say. This house had never been healthy *because* of the people in it. "I suppose."

"We live across the street in the beige brick with the black shutters. I'm Davis Turner and these are my munchkins, Paige and Nathan."

Lana released a tiny inner sigh of relief. Davis didn't recognize her, though sooner or later he'd discover he lived too close to the town bad girl.

Would the people of Whisper Falls still remember? Did she dare hope that time had erased her teenage indiscretions from inquiring minds?

Not a chance.

"I'm ten. Well, almost," the young girl at Davis's side announced. "Nathan's barely eight. I'm the oldest. What's your name?"

"This is Sydney," Lana said, purposely providing Sydney's name instead of hers. She couldn't avoid the introduction forever, but she wanted to buy some time before Davis's bright smile withered and he turned on his heels, dragging his children in a rush to lock his doors and keep them away. "She's also nine, just barely."

Sydney hung back, aqua eyes cautious. She was too shy, too hesitant with others, something Lana hoped would disappear once they were settled. Her niece needed friends badly and Lana prayed her prior reputation in this close-knit mountain community wouldn't interfere with Sydney's happiness.

"Say hello, Sydney."

Sydney ducked her head, displaying the precise part in her super curly brown hair. "Hello."

"Are you gonna live here?" the little boy, Nathan, asked.

"We are."

"Just the two of you?" With the same blue-gray eyes, brown hair and square jaw of his father, Nathan was handsome. Unlike his father, he sported a dimple in one cheek.

"That's the plan," Lana answered.

"Are you married?"

Paige elbowed her brother. "Shh."

"But Paige, we have to know," Nathan protested. "She has brown hair!"

The adults exchanged glances and smiled. Davis appeared as clueless about the comment as Lana. What did her hair color have to do with anything, especially marriage?

Paige, an elfin beauty, simple and pure with pale brown freckles and ultrashort blond hair, attempted to explain. "What he means, ma'am, is that we're glad to meet you and we'd like to get better acquainted. Isn't that right, Daddy?"

Davis turned his twinkly smile on Lana again, clearly amused by his children. "Always glad to welcome new neighbors. I didn't get your name."

The jig was up. She'd prayed to get settled before her tainted past charged in with all guns blazing. Apparently, God, Who'd brought her this far, expected her to face her fears head-on.

It was now or never. Either Davis remembered or he didn't. Time to find out.

Chin up, eyes meeting his, she said, "I'm Lana Ross. You and I attended high school together."

Davis blinked rapidly, off balance. This was Lana Ross? The wild child from high school? The girl with the bad attitude and potty mouth who was rumored to do about anything with anyone?

"I thought you looked familiar." But different, too. The hard-eyed teenager who'd run off to seek fame and fortune in Nashville looked softer as an adult. Lana had always been pretty, but the softer look made her beautiful. Long, brown hair waving past her shoulders, dark mink eyebrows above clear eyes the color of the Tuscan blue tile he'd installed in a recent boutique remodel, cowboy boots over skinny jeans and an off-shoulder blouse on a petite form.

Pretty. Real pretty.

Davis was disturbed to feel a pull of interest.

Considering the welfare of his children, he wasn't even sure he wanted Lana Ross for a neighbor. He certainly didn't want to be attracted to her.

His conscience dinged, a sign the Lord was knocking on his door. *Let you without sin cast the first stone.*

Right. He agreed. He was no better than anyone else. But what about his kids? He was a firm believer in the old adage, "If you run with the wolves, you'll begin to howl." As a single father, he struggled to find exactly the right parenting balance, but he certainly didn't intend to have howling children.

"Daddy." Nathan tugged at his sleeve. "Can we go inside? Can we explore the haunted house?"

Lana arched an eyebrow at him. A little embarrassed, Davis said, "Sorry about that. You know how kids are. The house has been empty such a long time…."

"And it *is* spooky looking, Daddy," Paige said, eyes widening. "I looked in the windows before and didn't see no headless horsemen or creepy monsters, but Jaley says they only come out at night."

Jaley was Paige's best friend, a child with a vividly overactive imagination. He could, however, understand why the house had gained a reputation. Peeling paint, sagging doors and filthy dormer windows that looked out like empty eyes through faded black shutters were creepy enough, but the overgrown bushes and vines and the sheer loneliness lent an air of doom to the place. More than one shaky teenager had been caught climbing in through a window on a dare.

But Paige's comments had scared Lana's little girl. Small like Lana with kinky curly beige hair, Sydney had stiffened, growing paler with each spooky word. She clung to Lana as if she was now afraid to go inside the house.

Davis put a hand on his daughter's shoulder and squeezed, the signal he used in church to get her to stop talking. Paige hushed, shoulders slouching as her bottom lip protruded. She'd gotten the message.

"The house is not haunted," he said firmly. "I told you that. Houses get lonely. All this one needs is a family." And an enormous amount of work.

"Now it has one," Lana declared, relief in her husky voice, though she tugged Sydney closer to her jean-clad thigh and soothed the child with a pat on the back.

"She'll need some fixing up," Davis said. "You know how some teenagers are when they know a house sets empty."

He'd caught a few of them himself, usually on nights with a full moon or late in autumn just before Halloween when wind and dry, rustling leaves permeated the atmosphere.

Lana blanched, eyes widening as she swiveled her head toward the peeling paint and loose siding and then back to him. "The house has been vandalized?"

Hadn't the woman considered the possibility?

"I haven't been inside in a couple of years, since before your mother passed, but things had run down even then." He didn't say the obvious. Patricia Ross had two daughters and neither had come home to help their ailing mother. He couldn't imagine being that coldhearted against your own kin. But then, Lana and Tess Ross hadn't been the usual girls. Patricia's brother had come from Nevada to bury her.

"Vandals," Lana murmured, looking as if the weight of the house was on her shoulders. "Wonder what that will cost to repair?"

Regardless of his doubts about her, Davis's natural compassion kicked in. He could help her out. He had the expertise. He *was* her neighbor. He fought the urge, but kindness won out in the end. Might as well give in to it now and save wrestling with his conscience later.

"I could take a look around the place if you want

and give you a rough estimate." That was all he planned. Just a quick walk-through.

"You do that sort of thing?"

The warm autumn wind lifted a lock of her hair and swirled it around until she had a spiderweb of brown matted on top of her head. She brushed at the nest, making it worse. He found the look charming and vulnerable. Davis was a sucker for vulnerable.

Tough-as-nails Lana Ross, vulnerable?

"I can," he said. "Mostly, I lay tile but I've flipped a house or two. I can do a little of everything when the situation calls for it." His face relaxed in a self-mocking grin. "In tile work, especially around here, the situation almost always calls for it. If I redo a shower, the floor beneath is inevitably rotten. Tile a floor? Bad joists."

For the first time since his arrival, Lana's pretty mouth curved. Just a little. "A true renaissance man?"

"Nowhere near that interesting, but I do know my way around a construction site."

Renaissance man. Huh. Funny. Except when he had a trowel or a hammer in hand, he was as boring as vanilla pudding. Didn't his sister remind him of that fact at least once a month? Jenny was forever trying to get him out into the world again. The dating world.

"Thanks for the offer, Davis," Lana was saying, "but I guess we need to get settled in first and then figure out where to go from there."

"Got it. Good plan." She was blowing him off, rejecting his offer. Even though disappointment made his smile droop, Davis knew he should be glad about her refusal. He'd have no obligation now, no guilty conscience for not being neighborly to a woman and her daughter living alone.

Which brought him to another subject: Where was Sydney's father?

As soon as the question settled in like good grouting mud, another followed. She'd never addressed Nathan's oddball question about being married, and she and Sydney were moving in without any sign of a man. Recalling Lana's teenage years, Davis thought the chances were very good the two were alone.

Chapter Two

"He was nice," Sydney said.

Lana absently stroked a hand over Sydney's frizzy hair as they stood on the top porch step—the only porch step—and watched Davis Turner and his kids recross the quiet residential street. A vanilla breeze danced around their feet, tossing leaves and dirt over their shoes and into a growing pile against the siding.

Davis *was* nice, but she'd seen the shock in his eyes and felt the temperature drop when she'd told him her name. He remembered.

Nothing she hadn't expected but still the reaction stung. She'd changed, thank God, the day she'd stumbled into a Nashville street mission drunk as a skunk after getting turned down for an important gig at the Opry. She hadn't known it then, but both had been her last chance. She'd never sung in public again, but she'd found the Lord and started on a new path.

Lana looked at Sydney, her throat aching with love and guilt. "Maybe you can be friends with Paige and Nathan."

Dear Lord, don't make Sydney pay any more for Tess's or my mistakes. Let this work. *Make* it work for her sake.

"Will Paige be in my class at school?"

"Probably. Maybe. I don't know. We'll have to ask. Come on, let's get the car unloaded." She thumped the flat of her palm against the center pillar in a show of energy she didn't feel. They still hadn't worked up the nerve to go inside the forlorn two-story, but they were here and they would stay. Regardless. Somehow she and Sydney would turn this dreary old relic into a real home, clearing out one room and one old ghost at a time.

"Nathan was nice, too," Sydney said. She reached her skinny arms into the backseat of the old Ford and dragged out a cardboard box. "He said I could swing on his swing set sometime."

"He did?" Lana had not even noticed the children talking, probably because she'd been too focused on their handsome father. Boy, did she ever remember *him!*

"Uh-huh. He did. So, can I?"

"We'll see."

"Paige said they have a dog. Can we get a dog?"

"I don't think so." When she saw Sydney's expression, Lana hurried to say, "Maybe later after we're well settled."

Sydney shoved the box onto the grass with a grunt. "Am I staying at this school forever?"

"Poor baby." Lana squatted for a hug. Sydney had changed schools frequently enough to develop reading difficulties. Lana was determined to remedy that problem this year. Stability was the answer, even if it meant living in this awful house. "We're going to try."

Sydney rested her hands on Lana's shoulders, face close. She had the most beautiful olive skin and turquoise eyes.

"You're not going to sing no more? Never?"

The loss was still as sharp as a hot stick in the eye. Music was the only thing Lana had ever been good at, though like everything else, not good enough. "No, baby. I have a real job now."

"Oh, yeah. I forgot." Sydney screwed up her face, feathery dark eyebrows drawing together over her nose. "What was it?"

"I'll be working for the Whisper Falls newspaper." She popped the lid on the trunk. Their pitiful possessions were stuffed into two cardboard boxes and a couple of battered suitcases. "I'll have press passes which means we'll get to go to lots of fun events for free. Football games, carnivals, plays, all kinds of things."

"Cool."

Actually, she was a stringer covering local events for the small paper. The pay was minimal but it was money. Along with the amount her mother left behind—unintentionally, Lana was certain—they should be all right for a while. That is if she could figure out how to write an acceptable article. School hadn't exactly been her thing, but like singing she could always write. She'd written lots of songs, none of which had been picked up, of course.

Joshua Kendle, the newspaperman on the other end of the telephone, had promised on-the-job training and hired her sight unseen, so how hard could the reporter job be?

Desperate times meant desperate measures. She would personally hand deliver every paper in town—or live in this house—to give Sydney a normal, stable life.

Sydney, slender back bent in half, began pushing a cardboard box across the grass.

"Hold on and I'll help you." Lana slammed the trunk of the dependable old Focus with one hand while balancing yet another box on her hip. Though she mourned the loss of her pickup truck, the Focus had been more economical and more sensible.

"I can do it by myself."

Box on one hip, Lana grabbed the smaller of the suitcases and rolled it, bumping along behind Sydney as she crossed the dry brown grassy distance from the cracked driveway to the porch. Times like these she could use a man around to help out.

Her thoughts shifted again to Davis Turner. She'd had a mild crush on him in high school though he'd never known it. He was an upperclassman, the boy everyone liked because, unlike his sister Jenny, he didn't have a snarky bone in his body. She wondered if he was still that way.

Time hadn't damaged his appeal. That was for certain. If anything, maturity had made him more attractive. Very Matt Damon-ish, and hadn't she always had a crush on the fresh-faced actor?

Lana shook her head in disgust. Men had been her downfall one too many times. Now that she had Sydney to consider and she no longer drank, she wasn't going down that road again.

Arms full and Sydney nowhere in sight, she kicked the storm door with her boot toe and caught it on the first bounce, thrusting it open with the rolling luggage. The door swung out and back quicker than she'd expected, catching her in the backside and knocking her off balance. The cardboard box tumbled from her arms, spilling its contents. In a juggle to stop her fall, Lana caught her boot on a loose piece of threshold and hit her knee against the suitcase. The rollers spun the bag in front of her, entangled her feet, and down she went.

Dusty carpet came up to kiss her. The musty odor of disuse and grime tickled her nostrils. Inside her childhood home for the first time in thirteen years and here she was sprawled flat on her face. With her underwear spread all over the floor.

Lips twisting wryly, Lana lifted her head and looked around. Crude red graffiti scrawled across the wall directly in front of her. She glanced to the right and then to the left. More graffiti. She shuddered and buried her face in the crook of her arm, breathing deep the lonely, musty smells. The buoyant hope that had propelled her four hundred miles scuttled away with the sound of whatever vermin roamed her childhood home. For the first time since the idea struck, Lana questioned her decision to bring Sydney to this house.

Maybe she should have let Davis have a look around after all.

Davis slid a pan of lasagna from the oven with a fat maroon oven mitt. The warm oregano scent filled his modern kitchen. He set the casserole dish on an iron trivet, careful to protect the gleaming black granite countertops he'd installed himself. If there was anything Davis enjoyed, it was transforming the looks of a room with tile and granite.

"Come and eat!" he called and was gratified to hear the scramble for the remote as one of the kids shut off the Wii game. "Red velvet cake for dessert."

Thank the good Lord for a sister who occasionally took pity on him and sent over dessert. He'd learned the basics of cooking but baking was out of his league. Jenny said a trained monkey could learn to follow instructions on the back of a cake box. Which Davis figured disproved the theory of evolution once and for all since he, a human, couldn't successfully manage the task.

"Did you wash your hands?" he asked when Nathan, forehead sweaty from the active boxing game, plopped into his chair at one side of the polished ash table.

Fingers stretched wide, Nathan held his palms up for inspection. "See? All clean. They smell good, too. Want to sniff?"

Davis scuffed his son's hair, affection welling in his chest. "Good enough for me, bud. Who wants to pray?"

"I will," Paige said, her face suddenly radiant as if transfigured by the idea of talking to God.

That was his daughter. She had an ethereal faith, disconcerting at times when she offered to pray for total strangers. "All right. Go for it."

They bowed their heads. Davis kept one eye open, trained on Nathan who had a habit of sneaking food into his mouth during prayer. Today, he was as pious as his sister.

"And Jesus, thank you for sending us new neighbors," Paige was saying. "Bless them and I hope they have plenty to eat, too, just like we do. Do you think they like red velvet cake? Amen."

Frowning, Davis turned his gaze on his daughter. Her sweet prayers never failed to move and impress him, but today he suspected an ulterior motive. "What was that about?"

"Well." With studied innocence that he didn't buy for one second, she took a slice of buttery garlic bread from the offered plate. "The Bible says to love our neighbor. Right?"

Davis looked down at the lasagna dish, suddenly uncomfortable. He suspected where this was headed. "Right."

"Lana and Sydney are moving in that old haunted house. They might not have any groceries in the fridge yet. They might not even have peanut butter and jelly sandwiches!"

"Or Popsicles," Nathan said. To Nathan, a Popsicle was one of life's necessities.

"A house without a Popsicle is a sad house indeed," Davis said, amused. He dolloped ranch dressing onto his salad and forked a bite.

"Anyway, Daddy," Paige said. "I was thinking. We want to love our neighbors and invite them to church and everything, right?" She jammed a glob of lasagna into her mouth while awaiting his reply.

Davis skirted the issue momentarily. "Nathan, put some salad on your plate."

Nathan's square shoulders slumped, a picture of dejection. "Aw, Daddy."

"Nonnegotiable. No salad, no cake."

Nathan reached for the salad.

Paige put down her fork. "Daddy, are you listening to me?"

"Sure, princess. What is it?"

"Are we going to take some lasagna and cake over to Lana and Sydney?"

Davis eyed the long casserole. They'd barely made a dent in the cheesy dish.

"I don't know, Paige. They might be busy getting settled." Lana had said those very words. They needed time.

"Everybody has to eat."

"She's pretty, isn't she, Daddy?" This from Nathan who was clearly avoiding the three tomatoes lined up like British redcoats on the edge of his plate.

"Who?"

"Lana. I think she's real pretty. Her hair is pretty, too. I like brown hair."

Davis swallowed. The forkful of noodles stuck in his throat. He grabbed for his water and swigged.

Yes, Lana was pretty. She and her sassy boots had been prancing around in his head the entire time he was cooking supper. He was curious about her, wondered why she'd left her life in Nashville and what secrets lurked behind her cool blue eyes. He wasn't sure he wanted answers, but he wondered.

He'd taught his kids to do the right thing, to treat people the way they would want to be treated, and that included greeting new neighbors. He was head of the neighborhood welcome community and co-chair of block parties and summer cookouts. Might as well find out early if Lana Ross and her child were people he wanted his children associating with.

"After dinner, if you kids will help clean the kitchen without grumbling, we'll take a couple of plates down the block. How does that sound?"

"You are the best daddy ever," Paige said.

"Yeah," Nathan added, nodding sagely. "Everything is going exactly like we planned."

"Nathan!" Paige shot him a paralyzing look and shook her head. Nathan clapped both hands over his mouth.

Davis looked from one child to the other, puzzled.

What was that all about?

Chapter Three

Beware of really handsome men bearing gifts.

These random thoughts ran through Lana's head as she tried to find a clean place in her filthy, run-down, pathetic kitchen to put two foil-covered plates.

Davis Turner was every bit as nice as she remembered. He'd brought food. Something she had not yet bothered to think about. Her stomach rumbled at the spicy, warm smells coming from the dishes. When was the last time she'd eaten anything healthy, much less homemade lasagna? She'd fed Sydney burgers and breakfast burritos on the road but had been too uptight to eat since yesterday.

"Sorry everything is a mess. The house is worse than I'd expected." A lot, *lot* worse. Apparently, Mother had let the place go and the years of sitting empty had taken a worse toll.

"You've got your work cut out."

"Don't I know it? I didn't expect it to be this

bad." She grimaced. "Or to have graffiti on the living room walls."

"Is the living room the only place that bad?"

"Seems to be. I guess vandals haven't gotten much farther than the front of the house. Hopefully, a good cleaning will make a big difference."

"What about the holes?"

"Not sure yet. Put something over them, I guess. Sydney and I decided sleeping quarters were number one, so we started on her bedroom first. We can camp there for a while." She didn't add that she'd camped in worse.

The three kids bumped around inside the small kitchen. Pixielike Paige, the oldest and clearly the leader, said, "Sydney wants to show us the upstairs. Can we go?"

"Lana may not want a bunch of kids traipsing through her house."

Lana gave a wry laugh. "Nothing they can hurt. Let them go."

At a wave of Davis's hand, the three kids took off in a rush, pounding up the wooden steps. Sydney was eager to share her room, such as it was, and Lana suspected the other two wanted to explore the "haunted house." She didn't hold it against them. She'd have done the same thing as a kid.

"Are the stairs secure?" Davis glanced toward the front of the house, though the entry stairwell was invisible from here. The kitchen was an add-on to the 1910 dwelling and as such, ran lengthwise across the back of the house where it met with the back porch. Long, narrow and inconveniently arranged, the kitchen could use some serious modernizing. Someday.

"We've been up and down quite a few times and I've not noticed any loose boards or weak areas."

"Good. Stairs can be an issue in older homes."

"These are sturdy oak, I think. Anyway, that's what I remember." Not that she'd paid much attention to the house other than her attempts to get out of it as often as possible.

"The place appears to have good bones. Old houses usually have better construction materials than newer ones unless there's dry rot."

"I hope that's true in this case." She shoved a bundle of old newspapers, yellowed with age, off a bar stool and onto the floor. "Have a seat?" she asked, not altogether sure he'd want to.

"Sure." To her relief he didn't seem all that bothered by the dirt and grime. Truth was she'd lived in worse. So had Sydney, bless her sweet, accepting soul. At least here in Whisper Falls they had a roof over their heads that no one could take away. Eventually, things under that roof would be clean and tidy and hopefully, free of the past.

"I'm glad you came over. Really glad," she started, twisting her hands on the back rung of a wooden chair. She was still amazed he'd returned after learning her identity. "I've been thinking about you." Her face heated. "I meant I was reconsidering your offer."

During the past few hours of bagging trash and scrubbing, she'd thought about Davis Turner. Beyond the fact that her skin sizzled when he'd smiled and her blood had hummed when she'd opened the door and found him standing there again. She wasn't too happy about *noticing* him so much, but she did need his help.

"I could use your expertise. I have a little money put aside. Not a lot but enough to address the most important needs of the house." She bunched her shoulders, aware of the knot forming at the base of her neck. She'd have a doozy of a muscle spasm if she wasn't careful. "Other than covering the holes in some of the walls, I don't know what those are."

"I can look around, make a list, give you some advice if you think that would help."

"Would you?"

"Sure. No problem. Got a pencil and paper handy?"

"Now?"

"No time like the present. That is, if now works for you."

"Of course. Thank you. Now is perfect." If she could find a piece of paper.

Feet pounded on the floor above their heads. Both adults raised their eyes toward the ceiling.

Lana was poignantly aware of the oddity of having Davis Turner in her house. He wouldn't have been caught dead here as a teenager. He'd been a Christian, raised in church, the boy teachers and parents put on a pedestal as the way all teens should behave.

Lana Ross had been his antithesis.

"What are they doing?" Lana asked.

"Don't know but that floor is solid or we'd be covered in ceiling plaster." He flashed that smile, lighting up the dim room.

The man had a killer smile. And two kids. It suddenly occurred to her that he'd never mentioned a wife. But then, half the world was divorced. She supposed he was, too, or his wife would have accompanied him on this neighborly expedition.

Lana rummaged around in the kitchen drawers, not surprised to find a dusty pad and a scattering of stubby, round-point pencils. Mother had always kept them there.

Davis took the writing materials and rose. He was considerably taller than her, even in her high-heeled boots, and filled the narrow kitchen with his masculine presence. Her awareness factor elevated. Above the kitchen's dust and must, he smelled of men's spice—just the faintest whiff but enough for her foolish female nose to enjoy.

Focus on the mission. Think of Sydney.

Even if she hadn't had a date in two years, Davis Turner was way out of her league.

They started through the house talking about the structure and basic needs, as well as noting cosmetic needs. After a bit, the kids came thundering down the stairs, a breathless chattering group that made Lana's heart glad. Sydney's happy face said it all. She'd made friends. Being back in this awful house just got easier.

"Can we go out in the backyard?" Paige asked. "Sydney said there was a cellar."

The cellar. Like a giant vacuum, the word sucked the pleasure from the room. "Stay out of that cellar."

Her sharp tone stopped the children in their happy tracks. "Why?" Nathan's eyes widened. "Is it haunted?"

Lana rubbed her suddenly cold arms. She hated that cellar, hated the darkness, the damp musty odor and the creepy crawlies inside. "I haven't cleaned it yet. Spiders, snakes, who knows what could be in there?"

"Eww. I don't like spiders." Paige shivered. "Can we go outside and play in the yard? Sydney said there's an apple tree."

Lana nodded. "Go on. Have fun but watch out for anything broken or dangerous. I haven't explored out there yet."

"Okay."

With youthful energy, voices excited, the trio zipped out the back door, leaving it standing open, spilling the sunshine and cool, clean air of Indian summer inside. Lana didn't bother to close it. She wanted to keep a watch on Sydney. Airing the house while the weather was favorable wasn't a bad thing either.

"Your children are really sweet."

"Thanks, so is yours. They're great kids, though they can be a handful at times. Paige has, shall we say, ideas that sometimes lead her and her brother into trouble."

Lana didn't bother to correct his mistake. It was better for everyone if he and the town assumed Sydney was her child. "But Paige seems like such a nice little girl."

"She is. I don't mean that." He hunkered down to look up into the fireplace. "Don't light this until it's been inspected and cleaned."

"Okay. I heard noises up there. Probably birds."

"Or bats," he said with male matter-of-factness.

Lana crossed her arms as she gave the fireplace an uncertain look. "You would have to mention bats."

"Bats won't hurt you."

"Remind me you said that when I'm in traction with a broken leg from running out of the room."

He laughed at her, the corners of his eyes crinkling upward. "Tough Lana Ross afraid of a bat?"

He had no idea what he was talking about. She'd never been tough. She'd only pretended to be. "Don't tell Sydney, okay? She thinks I'm fearless."

He dusted his hands together. Dust motes danced in the sunlight streaming in from the window next to the big, old-fashioned brick fireplace. "My kids are the same. Nathan told one of his buddies I could pick up a house."

"So what happened? Did the kid come over and ask for proof?"

"Naturally."

"What did you do?"

"What else could I do?" His hands thrust out to each side. "I picked up the house."

The silliness made her laugh. This was the Davis she remembered. Self-effacing, warm, kind to anyone. Even her. "Be glad he didn't go for the 'my dad can beat up your dad scenario.'"

"I remember saying that when I was in elementary school."

"Like father like son?"

"Absolutely. But Paige is the same. Between the two of them, they slay me sometimes." He leaned the notepad against the fireplace brick and scribbled something on the paper. "A few weeks ago, the kids and I went up to Whisper Falls on a picnic. I made the mistake of falling asleep."

"What happened? Did they tie you to a tree? Douse you with water? Cover you with mayo?"

"Nothing that simple for those two. They climbed Whisper Falls."

"No way!" Lana glanced out the grimy window at the two Turner children running across the thick brown grass. Whisper Falls was a long, slippery climb, especially for two small children. She should know. She'd climbed it plenty, usually on some stupid dare or when she'd had too much beer to be walking, much less climbing. "Why would they do that?"

"Paige says they went up there to pray. I suppose you've heard the rumor about praying behind the falls."

"The moment I hit town, but it must be a new thing. No one said that when I lived here before. What started it?"

"I'm not sure. Some say Digger and Evelyn Parsons made up the story. Others say they've actually had prayers answered after going up there. Someone got the city council on board and they changed the name of the town to match the waterfall. Next thing we knew, tourists started making pilgrimages up the mountain."

"Do you believe it's true?" Because if it was, she was climbing those falls again. This time without a party—and stone cold sober.

"A rumor of that caliber is good PR, but I don't think God needs a waterfall to answer prayers, do you?"

So, he was still a Christian.

"I agree, but maybe your daughter doesn't."

"Paige." He huffed out a sound that was half frustration and half affection. "My daughter's faith is kind of hard to explain. Sometimes she's scary in the mature things she says about God. Other times she's a goofy kid, like that day. My heart stopped when I looked up and saw Nathan clinging like a spider monkey to the side of the mountain."

"What did you do?"

"What else could I do? I climbed up after them. Once we were on the ground, I hugged them, told them how scared I was and how much I loved them. Then I grounded them both from TV for a full week."

Lana laughed. "You are a cruel father."

"They thought so." He stuck the stubby pencil in his shirt pocket and started across the room. His long legs ate up the floor, even though the parlor was large. "All the while, Nathan kept saying the oddest things."

Lana followed his lead, taking a left down a dim hallway. "Such as?"

"Nothing specific. Random things about brown hair." He tapped on the paneling, made a note of loose trim and a cracked light fixture.

"Sydney once asked me to dye her hair green, but that was for a costume party." Lana opened the door to the downstairs bathroom, a small space with an old claw-foot tub.

"Nice." Davis ran a hand along the rounded edge. He didn't seem to mind that it was filthy. "Do you know what these sell for in today's market?"

"If it's more than a new one, this one is for sale."

"Seriously?"

"I've had old stuff all my life, Davis. All these antique fixtures can go for all I care."

"I'll check around. You might be able to make some money. Lots of people like authentic vintage."

The idea heartened her. She and Sydney would make it here. She would find a way to turn this house into a home.

"Tell me about yourself, Lana," he said, tapping the wall above the bathroom sink with his knuckles. "What happened to your singing career in Nashville?"

"You knew I lived there?"

"This is Whisper Falls. We hear everything. Usually, about five minutes after it happens."

He was right, and the memory of a small, gossipy town was not a comfort. People would remember her teen years. People would gossip. All she could do was pray the talk didn't harm Sydney. There would be enough speculation about her as it was.

"So what about Nashville?" He leaned forward to inspect the hot water tank. Other than being coated in dust and cobwebs, it worked. She knew that already.

"The usual, I guess. I thought I was a better singer than I am. But I had some great experiences." Some lousy ones, too. "I sang for my supper, met some famous stars." Usually at the hotel where she'd cleaned rooms, though she'd once encountered Faith Hill and Tim McGraw coming out of Banana Republic with their kids.

"I remember when you and your sister used to

sing the national anthem at the football games. You were good. Where's Tess living now?"

That was anyone's guess. Under a bridge. In a crack house. But hopefully, in the same mission that had brought Lana to Christ. "She's still in Nashville."

The conversation was beginning to take an uncomfortable turn. Lana didn't want to discuss Tess or Nashville for that matter.

"You've lived a glamorous life. Why come back to Whisper Falls?"

Glamorous? "Time to settle down. Sydney needs to be settled in one place, one school, and the music industry is not always a stable lifestyle. Anyway, it wasn't for me."

"I get that. My kids are everything. I'd walk on fire for them."

"Or climb Whisper Falls?" Lana asked, surprised at the easy joke.

"Exactly."

He opened the vanity cabinet. A dead mouse smell rushed out.

"Eww." Lana grabbed her nose and backed out of the small space into the hallway. Davis, more resourceful, leaned over the tub to shove open a tiny window. Fresh air, spurred by the breeze, swirled inside, but the stench remained. Outside, an overgrown pine scraped against the screen, dropping pine needles without enough scent to matter.

Davis followed her out into the hall, pulling the door behind him. "Let that air a while."

"Good idea. Maybe for a year."

"If you've got a plastic bag, I'll see if I can find and remove the source."

In the narrow hallway, they were crowded. If either moved more than a few inches they would be touching. Rather, she'd be touching that work-muscled chest of his. A man who carried boxes of tile and grouting mud had to be strong.

"You'd do that?"

Davis didn't seem to notice her discomfiture. He tilted his head, looking down at her while she looked up. "I work in remodels. You wouldn't believe some of the things I find behind walls and under old cabinets."

She squeezed her eyes shut and shivered in pretend horror, though the ploy was more to get her mind off him than true repugnance. "I don't think I want to know."

After he had dispatched the mouse carcass, for which she would forever be grateful, they made their way on through the house. Lana watched in dismay as his list of repairs grew longer and longer.

By the time they'd worked the way back to the kitchen, the kids came flying through the back door, faces red and sweaty.

"We're thirsty," Sydney said. "I wish we had some pop."

"Sorry, peanut. Water will have to do. It's all we have."

None of the trio looked all that thrilled with ordinary water but Lana scrubbed three glasses and filled them. They gulped it down and wiped hands across their faces.

Nathan, who was too cute for words, plunked his empty glass on the counter. Cheeks as red as a slap, he looked from Lana to Davis and said, "This is nice."

Paige grabbed his arm. "Let's go, Nathan."

"Why? I want to see if Daddy and Lana are having fun, too."

The little boy's comment amused and touched her, too. He was having fun. He wanted his daddy to have a good time, too.

"Nathan," Paige said urgently. "Let God do the work." She put her fingers to her lips and twisted in the classic gesture of turning a key in a lock. Whatever the boy was about to say, his sister wanted him to be quiet.

Nathan opened his mouth as if to protest but then closed it again. "Okay."

"Last one to the apple tree is a monkey's uncle," Paige said. And away they flew.

Lana cocked her head. "I wonder what that was all about."

"With those two, don't even ask."

"I think they're enjoying themselves," she said.

Thank you, Lord. Seeing Sydney carefree made the sacrifice of coming back to this town worth it.

"I wouldn't mind a glass of that water myself." Davis stuck his hands beneath the faucet and scrubbed. "I can wash my own glass."

"I'll do it."

"Too late." He stuck a glass beneath the spray and scrubbed. Then he filled and drank. With his hips leaning against the sink, he faced her. She could see he had something on his mind.

"Am I crazy for trying to live in this run-down old house?" she asked. "Is that what you're about to say?"

"What? No. Most of this is cosmetic." He waved a hand around in the air. "Structure is sound, plumbing is old but sturdy. Electrical box looks fairly new. Lots of work and a fair expenditure of money but livable."

Lana drew a deep breath through her nose. The knot in her neck eased. As much as she wanted to do this on her own, she couldn't. If she was alone, she wouldn't care where she lived. But Sydney mattered. "You're hired."

"Don't rush into anything. I'm pretty booked up right now with the holidays on the horizon, but I'll run some figures for you, work up an estimate, talk to other contractors. Then we'll need to talk budget."

"Small." She eased into a chair. "I want to

do most of the work myself, but some of these things…" She shrugged.

"There you go, then. Start there. Take this list." He handed her the tablet. "Figure out what you want to do yourself. Then sub out the rest to the experts. I can give you a list of those, too."

"You've been a lot of help."

"That's what neighbors do."

Neighbors? Really? Then where had they been years ago when she and Tess had needed them?

Chapter Four

The next evening after a long, fruitful day of work, Davis hurried up the sidewalk to his sister's home to collect his children. Jenny had been, quite literally, a godsend after Cheryl's death. A homeschooling, stay-at-home mom married to an accountant, she lived on the opposite side of town from Davis, which in Whisper Falls wasn't that far. Located in a newer addition along the bluff overlooking the Blackberry River, the speckled brick house had an aboveground pool in the backyard, closed now for the season, and a massive play fort that kept his kids enthralled for hours.

He let himself inside his sister's house which always smelled of candle scents and looked freshly polished. Every piece of furniture, every flower arrangement and picture was pristine. He marveled at how well Jenny managed with his kids and hers, including a son with health challenges, and two cocker spaniels.

"Anybody home?" he called, his usual announcement, and one that started the dogs barking.

"Daddy!" a joyful voice squealed. In seconds, Nathan came racing into the living room, a red superhero cape flying out behind him. He leaped into Davis's arms and wrapped his legs around his daddy's waist.

The weary workday melted away in the warm, exuberant little-boy hug from his son. His baby. The child he'd made with a woman he loved. He thanked God every day for his kids. They'd kept him sane when he'd wanted to curl into a ball and let go of life.

Though sometimes he still ached from the lonely spot Cheryl had left behind, he was a content man. Breathing deep, he held his son close to his chest, not caring that he was dirty and stained with grout. Life didn't get any better than the love of his sweet little boy and girl.

Jenny came around the dining room divider, smiling as she wiped her hands on a dish towel. Blonde and almost as tall as he, his sister had continued to gain weight after twin boys were born seven years ago. He thought she looked okay, but Jenny worried about being fat and was on some kind of crazy diet more often than not.

"You look bushed," she said. "Want to sit a while and have some tea?"

Davis shook his head. "Thanks, but no. Laundry to do tonight."

"You got a minute then? I want to ask you about something."

"Sure." He shifted, repositioning Nathan onto his hip. The boy's legs were starting to dangle like octopus tentacles, a sign he would soon be too big to leap into his daddy's embrace. Davis wasn't ready for that. "What's up?"

"The kids told me Lana Ross has moved back into her family's old house."

"True."

"They also said you'd been over to see her. Twice." He could see his sister was not happy about his friendliness. Never one to keep her opinions to herself, if Jenny had something to say, she'd say it. Sometimes that propensity was a good thing, but not always.

"True, as well. Being neighborly." He unwound Nathan's arms and let him slide to the floor. "Go get your sister, bud. We gotta go."

Jenny waited until Nathan skidded around the corner, spaniels in nail-tapping pursuit, before continuing. "Is Lana planning to stay in Whisper Falls?"

"I didn't ask her, but she's remodeling the Ross house. I figure that's a sign she's here for good."

"You're not going to get involved with *that*, are you?"

Her tone raised bristles on the back of his neck. "I might. Why?"

"Davis, don't you remember Lana Ross at all? What she was? How she was always in trouble, always doing the worst possible things? Surely, you aren't going to let your children associate with a woman like her."

Davis sucked in a chest full of air and tilted back on his boot heels. Jenny was protective of him and his kids, especially since Cheryl's death. Besides, hadn't he thought the same things about Lana?

"Come on, Jen, that was years ago. Teenagers do crazy things but they grow up."

"Maybe. But where has she been all this time? What has she been doing? Why would she come back here where everyone knows about her?"

"Maybe because she owns a house here?" he said with a hint of sarcasm, hands up and out. "I don't know."

"Don't risk your children to find out. Stay clear of her, Davis. She's a bad influence."

"Sis. Come on. Chill out. This is not like you. Lana is new in town. Even though she was born here, she's been gone for years. She's in my neighborhood."

"Which does not mean you have to associate with her. You have plenty of friends." She put a hand on his arm in a gesture of concern, her eyes worried. "Keep a nice, safe distance. That's all I'm asking."

"Too late for that. Nathan and Paige like her and her little girl. They're already begging to have Sydney to the house for a sleepover."

Jenny's head dropped backward as she gave an exasperated sigh. "That's another thing. Lana has a child. I'll bet you anything she isn't married. If she's like she was in high school, she probably doesn't even know who the father is."

Davis's jaw tightened. He loved his sister and appreciated her help, but she was taking this too far. In a deceptively quiet voice, he said, "Passing judgment, are we, sis?"

Jenny's chin went up. Her nostrils flared below pale eyes that arced fire. "Not in the least. Protecting our loved ones from harm is a Christian responsibility. Remember what Dad used to tell us about running with the wrong people? The Bible even warns against 'casting your pearls before swine.'"

"Wait a minute. Stop right there." She was starting to get under his skin. "Are you calling Lana a swine? You don't even know her."

"But I *remember* her. We had more than one run-in during high school." Jenny twisted the towel as if wringing Lana's neck. Or his. "I love your kids. I don't want them exposed to alcohol and drugs and Lord only knows what else. Do you want them to have a reputation like those awful Ross sisters?"

"They're in grade school, for crying out loud! Come on, Jenny. You're being ridiculous."

And she was making him uncomfortable. Hadn't he struggled with these same, ugly thoughts yesterday? Yet, Lana and her little girl gave no sign of being anything but decent people. Even if they weren't, didn't God expect him to show grace and charity?

But he wanted to protect his children, too.

While brother and sister stared each other down and Davis wrestled with his thoughts, Nathan and Paige entered the room, followed by seven-year-old twins Charlie and Kent. The boys were apple-cheeked replicas of their dark-skinned father, though Charlie was smaller and wore a pallor lacking in his healthier sibling. Born with a heart defect, he'd had surgery soon after birth but he still took medication and had never been quite as vigorous as Kent. His condition was the main reason Jenny homeschooled. A valve replacement was in his near future, a fact that stressed the whole family, especially Jenny. Because of Charlie's uncertain health, Davis felt for his sister, but she could make him crazy, too.

"Ready?" Davis asked, grateful for the interruption to the contentious conversation. He was a peacemaker. Arguments made him miserable. Besides, his sister had enough on her plate. He didn't want to add to her worries by fighting over a woman neither of them knew that well.

But he was also a grown man, capable of making his own decisions and caring for his children. He didn't need his baby sister's dire warnings.

"Can we go see Sydney when we get home?"

Nathan asked, presenting a cupcake smashed inside a Ziploc bag. "I saved her half of my cupcake."

Jenny hissed, her glare burning a hole into her brother. "See?"

Davis ignored her. "That was really thoughtful of you, son."

"Paige saved *all* of hers for Lana." Nathan nodded sagely. "She has brown hair."

"My cupcake! I almost forgot." Paige clapped a hand against her forehead. "Wait a minute, Daddy, while I go get it."

His little girl hurried out of the room.

Jenny rolled her eyes at Davis. "Nathan has mentioned brown hair several times today. He even drew a picture of a woman with brown hair. What is *that* about?"

Davis shrugged. "Couldn't say. Why don't you ask him?" He dropped a hand on his son's shoulder. "What's the deal, Lucille? Why are you suddenly obsessed with brown hair?"

"Because," Nathan said, his voice exasperated as if Davis should understand. "Me and Paige prayed. God is going to send us a new mom with brown hair."

"What?" Davis exchanged stunned glances with his sister. This did not sound good.

"Don't you see, Daddy?" Nathan stretched his small arms wide, the smashed cupcake dangling in its bag. "After we prayed, Lana moved into the haunted house. Get it?"

A slow dawning broke through Davis's thoughts. "Was that why you climbed up Whisper Falls? To pray for a new mom with brown hair?"

Nathan slapped a hand over his mouth. "I wasn't supposed to tell. Paige says we have to let God do the work. We're just His helpers."

Davis squeezed the small shoulder in a gesture of comfort.

The kids had prayed. Lana Ross had moved in. She was single—and she had brown hair.

Naturally, their wild imaginations would take over and assume Lana was God's answer.

He raised his eyes from his son's dejected body to his sister's face.

"This is already getting out of hand, Davis."

He dragged a hand down his face and felt the rough dryness of tile glue still stuck to his fingers. "No kidding."

Jenny touched his arm. "Promise me you'll be careful, okay? You know what she is even if they don't. These kids have been hurt enough."

Davis's belly took a nosedive.

How could he argue with that?

Lana drove through the quiet, lazy town of Whisper Falls—past the train depot in the center town circle, past the Tress and Tan Salon, Jessup's Pharmacy, Aunt Annie's Antiques, and nearly drooled at the delights in the window of the Sweets and Eats candy store. The town didn't look as tired and run-down as it had when she'd left, when it had been Millerville.

"Look, Lana." Sydney, on the passenger side of the car, whipped her head toward Lana, eyes widened. "Sorry. I meant Mom."

Though Lana had been Sydney's primary caregiver most of her life, she'd never usurped Tess's title as Mom. Until now.

"You understand why it's important that everyone believe you're my daughter, don't you, peanut?"

Sydney nodded. "So I don't have to go to foster care."

"That's the gist of the matter. But if you slip up and say my name instead, we'll just pretend that's the way we do things. Okay?"

Pretending—or more accurately, lying—bothered Lana. She'd promised the Lord to change her bad habits but shading the truth was for Sydney's protection. Surely, God would agree the end justified the means when a child's well-being was on the line. Wouldn't He?

Sydney nodded though her expression was worried. "I remember what happened in Nashville when that woman came to school and asked me all those questions about you and Mama and where we lived. I was real scared. I thought I might never see you again."

Lana reached across the console to pat her niece's knee, taking note that Sydney didn't worry about the loss of her birth mother. She worried about losing the aunt who'd raised her. "I know, baby. That's why we're here now. Nobody is going to take you away. Not ever."

"You won't let them, will you?"

"No." *Not as long as I have breath in my body and legs that can run.*

Because of Tess's constant run-ins with the law, the child protective agency had investigated Sydney's living situation. The interview at school had been a warning to Lana that she might lose Sydney if she didn't take action. So she had. With her own less-than-stellar background, she feared social services would reject her as well as Tess—the reasons she and Sydney had come to Whisper Falls, the one place Lana had never wanted to see again.

"I didn't mean to tell my teacher about living in the car. It just kind of slipped out when she asked about making a fire escape plan for our house."

"It's okay. You're safe. We're going to have a good, good life in Whisper Falls." *No matter what it takes.*

"Are we having Christmas here?"

"Christmas?" Lana said, laughing softly. "We're barely into November."

"But look." Sydney's nail-gnawed fingertip pecked against the passenger window.

City workers high on the "cherry picker" lifts normally used to change streetlights, strung Christmas decorations across the short five-block main street. Christmas. She was always amazed how quickly the holiday arrived once October slipped away. With Thanksgiving on the horizon, Christmas, and winter, would be upon them before she could get the house in shape.

Unless she enlisted considerable assistance.

Her thoughts flashed to Davis Turner. He'd actually made her feel welcome as if her ugly reputation wasn't dancing around inside his head. As if she would be accepted in her old hometown.

He'd given her hope.

With Sydney jabbering about Christmas and wondering if Paige would be in her class at school, Lana drove through town, turning down a side street and into a residential area that led to the school. A long, low, redbrick complex of buildings and facilities, the school had grown considerably since her days of skipping class to smoke in the gym locker room.

But Jesus had wiped her slate clean. All she had to do was convince the rest of the world she'd changed.

Tall order.

She parked the car and went inside the elementary school, holding Sydney's hand. Lana's own palm sweated, though the temperature wasn't overly warm as they stepped through the door marked Principal. Memories flashed. Detentions, threats, suspensions. Her own smirks and bad attitude. Not in this particular office, but in others like it.

Lord, she'd been a nightmare.

"May I help you?"

The woman behind the reception desk looked familiar. Lana glanced at the nameplate. *Wendy Begley.*

Choosing her words carefully, Lana said, "My little girl needs to enroll in third grade."

Wendy turned her attention to Sydney with a smile. "What's your name, honey?"

"Sydney Ross, ma'am. Are you the principal?"

"No, honey. The principal is up in the high school right now. I'm the secretary." Her eyes lifted to Lana. "I thought I recognized you. Lana Ross, right? Or is it Tess?"

"Lana."

"I don't know if you remember me. I was a few years behind you in school but I remember you and your sister, the infamous Ross girls." She gave a soft chuckle that held no rancor. "I used to be Wendy Westerfeld. Married Doug Begley. You remember him, don't you? His daddy owned the car wash. We have it now that Gordon retired."

"Oh, yes, of course." Lana did her best to appear bland and polite but inwardly she cringed. She remembered Doug all right. He'd been a party to a few of her self-destructive moments. "Do we need to fill out some paperwork to get Sydney enrolled?"

"Do you have her records from the other school?"

"Uh, no. We, uh, I—homeschooled her. We moved around a lot with my job." *Liar, liar. For-*

give me, God. "I have her shot record and birth certificate, though."

Before the other woman could inquire more deeply, Lana handed over the records.

Wendy took the documents to a file cabinet where she extracted a folder and a packet of papers. "Here is the enrollment packet. The paperwork is lengthy so you can take the whole packet home if you'd like and send it back with Sydney tomorrow."

Lana accepted the thick stack, thankful for the relaxed manner of a small-town school. Trusting and nice, and oh, she wanted to be worthy of both those things. "Sounds good. Thank you."

"All I need today is this top form of contact info, emergency numbers, that kind of thing. Will she be riding the bus?"

"We live in town. I'll drive her."

Wendy made a notation on the form. "Cafeteria or bringing her lunch?"

"Cafeteria for now. How much money does she need?"

Wendy named the amount and Lana paid for the week, relieved that the enrollment was going so well. She held her breath while the secretary made a copy of Sydney's birth certificate without so much as a glance at the parent's name and slid the copy into a folder.

One hurdle down.

Afterward, Wendy walked them down a long hallway decorated in happy primary colors and motivational bulletin boards to one of the third-grade classrooms to meet Sydney's new teacher.

With a final hug, Sydney hitched her Hello Kitty backpack and disappeared into the classroom. As the frosty-haired teacher closed the door, Wendy said, "Mrs. Pierce is a wonderful veteran teacher. Sydney will love her class."

"She's kind of shy."

"She'll be fine."

Lana's boot heels tapped against the white tile floor as they headed back toward the office. "You have children?"

"Four of the little boogers. Two, six, eight and ten." Wendy laughed. "That adorable two-year-old snuck up on us."

Lana laughed, too, relieved and grateful to Wendy Begley for her easy, welcoming demeanor. The school had chosen their secretary well.

She was beginning to think her return to Whisper Falls would not be as difficult as she'd imagined when another woman stepped into the office.

"Here's our principal now," Wendy said as she regained her desk chair. "Ms. Chester, do you remember Lana Ross? She just enrolled her daughter in third grade."

"Lana," the woman said coolly, slowly turning on black, shiny pumps, her suit the color of eggplant and her eyes as frosty as January. "How...interesting to see you again. What brings you back to this dull little mountain town?"

Lana's confidence, buoyed first by Davis's kindness and then Wendy's, now wilted like a daisy in the snow. She barely remembered this woman but clearly she'd been judged and found wanting.

The trouble was, she couldn't argue. She was as guilty as charged.

Lana left the school feeling lower than a snake's belly. Her fingers itched for her guitar and a chance to let the music melt away the disquiet in her chest. But she couldn't today. Today she had her first face-to-face meeting with her new boss, Joshua Kendle.

She drove to the newspaper office, past more of the quaint, picturesque mountain town she'd once wanted to escape. Even now, the need to run pressed in. Sometimes she was ashamed because the desire to get dog drunk and escape her problems almost overwhelmed her. Only the thought of how far she'd come, of how much God had done for her, and of Sydney, kept her straight and sober.

As she parked at an angle in front of the newspaper office, her hands trembled against the steering wheel. She took out her phone and punched in the speed dial number to Amber, her counselor at the mission in Nashville. After a brief conversation and prayer, she stepped out of the car with renewed courage. She'd come too far to turn back now.

Assailed by the scent of bacon, she spotted Marvin's diner, a familiar old haunt tucked in between the dry cleaners and an antique shop across the street from the *Gazette,* and smiled. Not everything in Whisper Falls had been bad. She could do this.

Head up, shoulders back, she marched through the half-windowed door into the *Gazette.* Immediately, the wonderful bacon smell gave way to printer's ink and old-fashioned type set that harkened to days gone by. The *Gazette,* it seemed, had yet to enter the full digital age.

"Morning. May I help you?" A short, potbellied man with sleeves rolled back on thick arms and wearing a backward baseball cap rounded a counter. He was probably in his early forties.

"I have an appointment with Joshua Kendle."

"You must be Lana." He scraped a hand down the leg of his faded jeans. "I'm Joshua. Welcome. You ready to get to work?"

Her shoulders relaxed at his affable warmth. "Ready. What do I do first?"

"Come meet the rest of the staff and then I'll show you the ropes." He took her through the back where several cubicles were set up with computers and introduced her to the small group of employees, including his wife, a heavyset blonde with big hair and a gold print scarf. "Hannah is the brains of the outfit. She handles the classifieds and subscriptions."

As Lana met the others, she relaxed more. No one here seemed to remember the awful Ross girls, or if they did, they didn't care.

After the introductions, Joshua led the way to his

desk crammed inside a tiny, messy office and got down to business, explaining Lana's duties and her pay-per-article salary. "Hannah gathers an events list from the schools, churches, civic groups, and posts it on the computer and out front on the bulletin board. You can access it yourself from home if you want. Attend as many of them as you can, write up a report, email it to me. I'll edit and proof and let you know if I have questions. Pick up your check every other Friday."

"That sounds too easy." Even if she hadn't written a full page of anything other than songs in years.

"You grew up in Whisper Falls, right?"

How did he know that? He wasn't a native. "Except it was Millerville back then."

"Your local knowledge should come in handy." Joshua didn't appear to be in a rush, but he moved and spoke quickly as if always on a deadline. Which in fact, he probably was. "This job will put you in contact with practically everyone in town at some point. It is a great way for you to get reacquainted."

She'd considered that, although she hadn't seen it as an advantage. Joshua might know she was a Whisper Falls native but apparently he knew little else. Thank goodness.

"You got a camera?"

"Only an old used one. The pictures are pretty good."

"That'll work. Simon is our staff photographer but he can't be everywhere. I use photos from anyone who'll send them in, so if you see something picture-worthy, take a shot, add a caption and email it to me. I'll go from there. If I use it, you get paid."

Awesome. "Okay."

"Good." He dug around in the mess of papers on his desk and pulled out a sheet. "Here you go. Friday night. Football play-offs. Give the kids a good write-up, mention lots of names so we can keep the mamas and daddies buying newspapers."

She wanted to ask how she was supposed to know who was who but held back. She needed this job. Any show of uncertainty on her part could kill the deal before she had a chance.

"I need the article by Saturday morning to make the Sunday edition. Can you do it?"

The offer, like the man, came fast and immediate. She hadn't been as ready as she'd let on. She'd planned to take some time and study back editions of the *Gazette,* to check out library books on writing.

But Joshua was waiting for her answer now.

She stuck her phone in her back pocket and tossed her hair with a fake smile. "Sure. First thing Saturday morning."

She'd write that article if she had to sit up all Friday night to do it.

Chapter Five

As Davis stood in the tool aisle at the Whisper Falls Hardware Store, he faced a dilemma. He was there buying a blade for his tile saw, a frequent expense, but he'd noticed Lana Ross leaving the store with two buckets of paint right after he'd arrived. Since the day he'd made a repair list inside her old two-story, he'd been thinking of his promise to help. He'd also been troubled by his sister's warning against getting too friendly with his new neighbor, especially since Nathan and Paige had some wild idea about matchmaking between him and Lana.

Brown hair. Good grief.

"That you, Turner?"

Davis swiveled to look at the newcomer, Pete Abernathy, a burly frame carpenter. They'd played football together in high school and frequently crossed paths in the construction business. "How you doing, Pete?"

"Good. Did you just see what I saw?"

"What was that?"

"Lana Ross. I heard she was back, but who would guess she'd look that good. Man! Eye candy." Pete smacked his tongue against his teeth, tsking. "You live close to the old Ross place, don't you? Did she move back in there?"

Irritation, like a gnat around the nose, buzzed along Davis's nerves endings. "Yep."

"I bet things are hopping around your neighborhood now."

"Not that I've noticed. She's a quiet neighbor."

"No way. Luscious Lana and her twin quiet? They were party central."

"That was a long time ago, Pete." His defense of Lana was starting to sound like an instant replay. And he wasn't even sure he was right. "So far, no parties. Just a lot of work on that run-down house."

"I heard she's single. No boyfriend. No husband. That true?"

"As far as I know."

"A shame. A woman like that alone. Figure she could use some *expert advice* from a willing man?" His tone indicated he wasn't discussing the Ross house.

Davis turned a cool gaze on the man. "Does your wife know you talk that way about other women?"

"Loosen up, dude. I didn't mean nothing by it. People talk. She's got a kid. I figured she's still a party girl." Flushing red, Pete yanked a saw blade from the rack and stalked away.

Davis watched him storm off, saw him muttering to the checker and suspected either he or Lana was the likely topic of conversation. With a sigh, he reached for an extra blade and headed to the checkout himself.

It didn't seem right that people would assume the worst about anyone, especially a woman they hadn't seen since the teen years. Sure, she'd been wild and crazy, but so had a lot of kids back then. Lana and Tess were known as the ringleaders, the party girls, always looking for trouble, but they never had to look far. There were plenty ready to run with them. Davis leaned toward a different crowd and had kept his nose clean for a couple of reasons. He'd been a Christian or had tried to be. He sure hadn't been perfect, but he'd wanted a scholarship. He hadn't gotten it and after a semester of barely making ends meet at college, he had ended up joining his dad's tile business. Much as the rejection had hurt when he was eighteen, he was content with his life today. For the most part.

On the drive to Jenny's to pick up the kids and then all the way home, he fumed over the conversation with Pete. For all he knew, Pete was right about Lana, and if people were already talking, her re-introduction to Whisper Falls might prove bumpy.

None of which was Sydney's fault. The little girl had crossed the street yesterday and invited his kids to play. She was a pretty thing, with bright eyes the color of the Hawaiian ocean and a sweet, gentle smile. He'd refused her request, using homework as an excuse.

He stole a glance in the rearview mirror at the kids in the backseat, heads together, focused on a handheld video game. Electronic zings and zaps mingled with their happy giggles. How would he feel if the neighbors snubbed them?

He was letting the opinions of others determine his actions when, in truth, Lana and Sydney had given him no reason to avoid them.

He was as big a jerk as Pete Abernathy.

As he turned down Dogwood Street into his neighborhood, he spotted the woman occupying his thoughts. His chest clenched. He ran a hand down the front of his T-shirt, pushing at the uncomfortable feeling.

In a pair of old jeans with one knee torn out and the hems frayed above white tennis shoes, Lana was standing on a ladder sweeping leaves from the gutters. One end of the gutter hung loose. A mishmash of building supplies was scattered on the porch.

Instead of turning toward his house, he pulled into Lana's driveway and got out. Both his kids hopped out, chattering like chipmunks.

When the car doors slammed, Lana turned her head. The brown hair that mesmerized his son was pulled back in a tail and held with a skinny red headband.

"Looks like you've got gutter problems," he

called. Not exactly scintillating conversation but an easy opening.

"I hope not." She frowned and glanced back to the roofline. "You think so?"

"Maybe not. If you'll come down I'll take a look."

"Would you?"

"Sure."

She was already backing down the ladder.

As he took her place, she said, "I'm trying to learn as much as I can about this remodeling business, but it's a sharp learning curve."

He squinted down at her. "YouTube?"

Her mouth curved. "How did you guess?"

"I've gone there myself a few times. There's some good advice and some really bad advice. Be careful." He tugged at the loose strip of gutter.

"What do you think?"

"The hangers need to be replaced but the fascia wood is in good shape."

"Are they expensive?"

"Under ten bucks apiece. An easy fix."

"Whew." Her face was tilted upward, so he was staring down at dark mink eyelashes that reached all the way up to equally dark eyebrows, the smooth, pretty curve of her neck and her full lips. "That's a relief. So far, it's the only thing less expensive than I'd hoped."

"What have you gotten done so far?"

"If you have a minute, I'll show you."

Davis twitched a shoulder. "Okay." He turned to

tell the kids, but they'd heard and were already on the porch, ready to barge in. "Hey, you two. Slow down," he said coming down from the ladder.

"Is Sydney home? Can she play?"

"She's inside doing homework."

"Which is where you two munchkins should be," Davis said, grabbing them both in a headlock from the back.

"Da-ad!"

"Please, Daddy, can we play for a minute while you talk to Lana?" She measured with her thumb and finger. "One teeny-weeny minute?"

"We can't stay long," he warned.

Taking that as a yes, they barreled inside and up the staircase, thundering like prairie buffalo.

"Sydney!" he heard Paige yell.

Lana laughed as they, too, went inside. "I'm beat from battling this house all day and they still have energy to run."

"Remodeling is a big job." He looked around the living room. "Nice. I didn't expect you to have the walls covered already."

She'd not only painted the ugly green walls and ceilings, she'd scrubbed the windows and fireplace and tossed sheets over the old furniture. The room was, at least, now livable.

Next to the fireplace, an acoustic guitar leaned against the wall, classic Lana. He remembered how good her voice had been. Anyway, she'd impressed their small town.

"I couldn't stand the graffiti," she was saying. "Some of the writing wasn't exactly family fare. I didn't want Sydney to read it."

"I hear that." And he liked it, too. If she didn't approve of rough language, she *had* changed. "The color is nice. Sort of a pale chocolate milk."

"I still have to paint the wood trim. What do you think of white enamel all around?"

"White's always nice. A good accent to the soft brown."

"That's what I was thinking, but the trim will have to wait until the true basics are done. Time has taken a toll on a lot of things, and the vandals didn't improve matters."

"Yeah, we should have done a better job of keeping watch after your mother passed."

"It wasn't your responsibility."

"Maybe not, but it was fun to catch those kids." He chuckled at the memory. "One night I saw a couple of shadowy figures sneaking around up here and decided to give them a scare."

"Did you really?" Her eyes sparkled with amusement. "What did you do?"

"There was this pair of teenage boys, probably 13 or 14. One was crawling through the kitchen window, the other hoisting from below." He pumped his upturned palms in a lifting motion. "I must have flashed back to my teenage days that night because I couldn't stop myself from what came next. It was too good an opportunity."

She cocked a hip, amused. "All right, spill it. I'm dying of suspense."

"Well, you see, it was dark. Barely a moon, and I had this chain saw." When she sucked in a knowing gasp, he grinned. "So, I carried it with me and hid behind a tree on the south side of the house. At the perfect moment, I jumped out screaming like a banshee and revved that chain saw for all I was worth."

Lana slapped both hands over her face and laughed. "You're kidding me? *You* did *that?*"

"Yep. Sure did. The kid in the window nearly knocked his brains out in his rush to escape. The one below took off in a screaming run and left his buddy hanging." The vision was as fresh in his head as yesterday and still cracked him up. "There he hung, with his legs dangling from the window and no way down except toward the chain saw."

"Oh, my goodness. That's priceless." She pointed her finger at him. "And exactly what they deserved for breaking into my house!"

"I laughed for days. Every time I thought about those big, brave, macho boys squealing like scared rabbits." He rubbed his hands together like an old-time villain. The tile glue made sandpaper sounds. "For a long time afterward no one bothered the spooky house on Dogwood Street."

"Davis Turner, you bad man. I had no idea you had it in you."

"You might be surprised at what I have in me,"

he said, and then wondered where that had come from and what he was talking about. Suddenly aware of how much he was enjoying her reaction to his tale, he grew self-conscious. "Well, okay then. Where were we?" He fisted his hands on his hips and stared around. "Oh, yeah, right. Working on the basics. Winterizing should be your priority this time of year."

She gave him a funny look, but followed along. "I bought caulk and weather stripping. Any other suggestions?"

"Pipes."

Her face fell. "You said the plumbing was solid."

"It is. I meant winterize the pipes."

"Oh. What does that entail?" Her top teeth gnawed at her bottom lip. He watched until it occurred to him that he was staring at her mouth. This was getting ridiculous. Instead of scaring him away, Jenny's pushiness had made him more interested.

"Any exposed plumbing needs to be wrapped or insulated in some way. The attic, crawl space, outside faucets." He saw her consternation at this latest addition to her growing list of repairs. "Not expensive. Just more work."

She blew out a breath. "Okay. Good. Work I can handle."

"Have you ever crawled under a house? That's the worst part."

She gave a little shiver. "Small, dark spaces don't rank at the top of my list."

"I don't think they're on anyone's list, but some people are bothered less than others. I don't mind too much. I'll have a look under there for you."

"You will?"

"It won't take that long." He hoped. A man had no idea what he'd encounter under an old house like this.

"I don't expect you to work for nothing. I'll pay you."

He waved off the suggestion. "We'll worry about that later."

"Speaking of lists, I've made mine."

He arched an eyebrow. "What list is that?"

"The things I can do myself. You offered to suggest subcontractors to do the rest."

"Oh, right, I did." His thoughts flashed to the frame carpenter in the hardware store. That was one subcontractor he would not recommend. "Got your list handy?"

"Always. It's on the kitchen counter, along with a general budget. Maybe you can tell me if I'm way off on the numbers."

She led the way into the kitchen. Little had been accomplished here other than a thorough cleaning. That in itself was a vast improvement.

"Let's see what you've got."

She handed over the list. "Do I have any hope of getting the house in decent shape before the colder weather arrives?"

"Hard to know. Could stay warm or could turn

bad." He leaned back against the counter to peruse the tidy hand-printed list. She'd used purple ink. "The lasting cold can't be far away though."

"I remember once when we were snowed in for two weeks. I thought I'd go crazy." She gave a soft, reminiscent laugh. "Tess and I finally bundled up in boots and coats, called a bunch of friends and trekked all the way up to Whisper Falls to go sledding on cardboard boxes."

"In the ice and snow? That's five miles." But it was the kind of thing the Ross girls would do.

"I've never been so cold in my life. One of the guys who came along finally built a campfire. We thought the smoke signals would bring out the fire department so we wouldn't have to walk back, but no such luck."

Davis nodded. "Remember that ice storm back in high school? Now that was cold."

"I remember. They called off school because the buses couldn't run, but those of us who lived in town were already there. Jack Macabee slid his VW off in a ditch and all of us piled out and lifted it back onto the road."

"I heard about that. You were in that car?"

She laughed again, stronger this time, and he could tell it was a good memory. "We must have had ten kids in that little Bug. All the boys thought they were strong enough to lift it out and Jack feared his dad would take his keys if anything happened to his car, so we got him going again. We slipped and fell, pushed and lifted, and laughed so hard." She leaned an elbow on the faded old countertop. "Whatever happened to Jack anyway? Did he take over his dad's car dealership?"

"No, Harvey closed the dealership when business disappeared to the bigger cities, but he still sells used cars on the side. Jack's a pumpkin farmer. You missed the Pumpkin Fest by only a couple of weeks. He was there in full force."

"Really? Pumpkins? I can't imagine preppy Jack in the agriculture business."

"It's kind of interesting to look at who we were then and where we are now. Life has a way of changing us."

"Isn't that the truth?" She'd gone pensive on him, bottom lip between her teeth, gaze somewhere in the distance. "I wouldn't want Sydney to be anything like I was."

"Aw, come on. Teenagers are goofy. You weren't so bad."

This time her laugh was harsh and disbelieving. "You always were the nicest guy. With an apparently faulty memory." She motioned toward the paper in his hand. "So what do you think? Any ideas for me?"

She was shutting off the conversation, unwilling to talk about herself anymore, but for a moment he'd glimpsed the young girl. He'd seen some things in her expression that surprised him. Hurt. Regret. Sadness.

Lana intrigued him. She also attracted him. He hadn't quite figured out why, other than his natural propensity toward the underdog and his sister's nosiness.

Troubled, he turned his attention to the list, though he was more aware of Lana Ross than he wanted to be. Her soft perfume played hide-and-seek in the narrow space. One minute, he caught the scent. The next it was gone.

He swallowed, bothered to be thinking about her, not as a neighbor in need as he'd told his sister but as a beautiful, interesting woman an arm's length away.

He cleared his throat. "You'll be putting in a lot of hours to do all this by yourself."

"I don't mind work as long as I can squeeze it in between my job."

The comment caught him off guard. He hadn't realized she had a job already. "Where are you working?"

"The *Gazette*." She glanced to one side, self-conscious and hitched a shoulder. "It's nothing big. A stringer position writing up local events. I get paid per article beginning tomorrow night."

"The football play-offs?"

Lana tilted her head. "How did you know?"

"Woman, the state play-offs are the biggest thing to hit the Whisper Falls Warriors in five years. Didn't you notice the signs plastered in all the businesses and the cars with Take State written on their back windows with shoe polish?"

"I guess you're right. Football fever has taken over and I don't even have a Warrior sweatshirt anymore."

"You'll have to remedy that."

"I will, but I've got bigger problems to worry about tomorrow night."

"What's that?"

"My boss, Mr. Kendle, wants an article filled with names. I don't know any of those kids. I might remember their parents, but not the kids."

"Easy fix. Get a spotter."

"A spotter?"

"That's what the announcers in the press box do. Someone sits up there with them and spots the numbers. They match the number to the program list and the problem is solved. The player gets recognized and everyone is happy."

"Perfect idea, but who? I'm still getting reacquainted."

"Well, let's see." He rubbed his chin, holding back the easy answer for two beats before saying, "How about me?"

Lana blinked, incredulous. "You?"

"Why not me?"

"Well, I, uh, I—" Rosy-red crested her cheekbones.

Davis lifted both hands. The paper crinkled, so

he put it on the table. "Hey, if that doesn't work for you, I'm okay with it."

"No, no, I would love for you to be the one." The blush deepened, a pretty sight on pale pink cheeks. "What I meant is, I don't want to impose. You've been so nice already."

"I haven't done anything, Lana. I'm going to the game anyway. If you want help, I'm in. If you'd prefer someone else, fine."

"I want you. There is no one else."

He didn't want to like the sound of that. "I'm expensive. You'll have to buy the popcorn."

"Deal. I might even throw in a bowl of chili."

Davis tossed the list onto the table and rubbed his hands together. "Chili, popcorn and the state playoffs right here in my own backyard. Gotta love it."

"I remember when you played."

"You do?"

"I sang the national anthem at every game from the time I was twelve. I was always there." She pulled the headband from her hair and smoothed the stray wisps, reminding him of Nathan's fixation on brown hair. "What was your number?"

"Twenty-eight. Running back."

Lana twirled the stretchy band in her fingers, playing with it. "You were awesome."

"So were you."

"Thanks."

Before he could pursue the titillating line of conversation, footsteps sounded on the stairs. Exchanging smiles, they both turned toward the doorway as three breathless, beaming children came running.

"How are things going, Dad?" Nathan's bright eyes moved back and forth between Davis and Lana. "Do you like her yet?"

Paige grabbed her brother's arm. "Nathan!" To Davis, she said, "Sorry, Dad. He's such a kid sometimes."

Davis exchanged a half chagrined, half amused glance with Lana. Her face was pink again, but her eyes gleamed as though she was holding back a laugh.

To the kids, he said, "Head for the truck, you two. We've got to go."

As soon as they disappeared, with Sydney trailing along, he said, "I apologize for my irrepressible son. I'll have a talk with him. As you might have guessed, he likes you."

Davis didn't add the rest—that her brown hair had made her the target of his children's Christmas matchmaking prayer. He wasn't sure he could handle the embarrassment or the uncomfortable yearning they'd ignited in him. A yearning he'd thought would never return after Cheryl's death. A desire he was, this moment, battling down like a bad cold.

If his sister could read his mind, she'd have him committed. He wondered what she'd say Friday night when she spotted him in the stands with Lana and Sydney at his side?

Chapter Six

Lana was sure she felt stares and caught a few double takes as she and Sydney passed through the gate at Warrior Field and stood behind the blue-and-gold streamer-laden goalposts soaking up the ambience of small-town football. She took a minute to look around, identifying familiar faces, scoping out the changes as well as the things that had remained the same.

Already in the stands, an overzealous drummer pounded a rhythm while the band warmed up. Flutes squeaked and tubas oomphed. On the grassy field, fresh-faced boys in shoulder pads went through their pregame warm-up ritual. Number seventeen called out drills that had the players falling to the ground and popping up to high-step in place a few seconds and then start the drill all over again. They counted out in a raspy chorus of adolescent male voices.

The stands were filling rapidly. Dozens of people

filed through the gate while buttery popcorn permeated the air with its alluring scent.

Lana shaded her eyes from the glare of the tall bright lights, searching for Davis. "Do you see Paige and Nathan yet?"

Sydney, giddy with excitement but clueless about football, shook her head. "Not yet."

"Hello, Lana."

Lana turned to see a familiar face. "Jack?"

Jack Macabee hadn't changed much other than some lines around his eyes. He still wore his golden-blond hair a little long and his eyes were still as green as grass. Tall, thin and lanky, he'd been a good basketball player. Tonight, he wore his high school letter jacket, as did many alumni, and it still fit him as well as it had thirteen years ago.

"I heard you were back," he said. "How's it going?"

"So far so good." Lana felt her shoulders relaxing. Just having a friendly face to talk to helped ease the strain of being in a new situation. She and Jack had gotten along pretty well way back when. "Davis Turner and I were talking about you the other day. He said you're a farmer now."

"Chief supplier to the pumpkin cannery," he said.

"That's great."

After that she wasn't sure what to say so they stood in silence until he asked, "Is this your little girl?"

"This is Sydney," she answered with a smile of agreement. "Do you have kids?"

"One. Ryan. He's ten. Since the divorce he lives with his mother in Fayetteville so I don't see him as much as I'd like. I get him every other weekend."

"That must be tough."

A look of resignation flashed. "You adjust to what you have to."

She certainly understood that and was about to say so when a hand wrapped around her upper arm.

A masculine voice muttered, "You got here first."

"Davis!"

The two men exchanged handshakes and began to talk about the Warriors' chances against their mighty rivals, the Longview Lions. After a brief conversation, Davis motioned toward the stands. "If we want a good spot, we'd better get up there. Want to join us, Jack?"

"Sounds good." He stuck his hands in his jacket pockets, an action that made him look like the youthful athlete she remembered. "Sure you don't mind?"

"Not a bit. Right, Lana?"

"Absolutely." She turned a genuine smile on Jack. Having another person along besides Davis's matchmaking kids provided more buffer and made her life easier. "The more the merrier as far as I'm concerned. It will be great to catch up again."

"I appreciate it. Since the divorce, I feel like the odd man out."

"I'm with you there," Davis said. "Being single again is awkward at times."

As they started forward, lost in manly conversation about offenses and defenses, Lana held back for a moment, thinking. The men were similar in many ways, though Jack's hair was more blond than sandy brown and he was much taller and thinner than Davis. It occurred to Lana that they had their bachelor status in common, as well. She'd never considered that a man who'd lost his wife, whether through death or divorce, might feel as much an outsider as she did.

Pondering this, she hoisted her writing tablet and shoulder bag and hurried to catch up. As the group moved down the sidelines and up the stairs into the bleachers, Lana occasionally heard her name in murmurs and whispers. Heat crept up the back of her neck, but she tried not to react. She'd expected gossip. This was, after all, a very small town. Everyone was fodder for gossip, especially the returned bad egg.

Suddenly, an older woman with a tight, salt-and-pepper corkscrew perm and a warm, bustling personality pushed up from a blue portable seat cushion boldly marked with a Warrior emblem.

"Lana Ross. Honey, is that you?" Clad in an oversize blue-and-gold Warriors jacket with matching earmuffs, Miss Evelyn Parsons waved a pom-pom on a stick directly at Lana. Of all the people in Whisper Falls, Miss Evelyn was one of the handful who never confused Lana with her sister. Though the twins were not identical, most folks didn't pay close enough attention to "those Ross girls" to notice the subtle differences.

"Miss Evelyn." Delighted, Lana stopped and accepted the hug, warmed by the best greeting she'd received so far. The Parsonses had always been kind, even after Tess had shoplifted from their snack shop.

"They tell me you're back and that you have the most adorable little girl." Miss Evelyn's gaze landed on the curious-faced child next to Lana. "This must be Sydney."

No surprise that Miss Evelyn, who made it her business to know everything possible about Whisper Falls and its citizens, had been informed not only of Lana's return but of her status as a parent.

"This is my darling girl." Lana touched Sydney's shoulder. "Say hello to Miss Evelyn, the matriarch of Whisper Falls. She practically runs the whole town."

"Especially me," said a portly man with white hair and handlebar mustache and a jolly chuckle. In his striped overalls and engineer's cap, Miss Evelyn's husband was a throwback to an earlier time, and he hadn't changed a bit since Lana had last seen him.

Lana smiled. "This gentleman is Uncle Digger. And before you ask, no, he's not your blood uncle."

"But he's everyone's uncle just the same," Miss

Evelyn said, patting her round, Santa-looking husband on the shoulder.

Sydney smiled her shy hello at both adults. "Hi," she said in a tiny, breathy voice.

"Lana, she is a *darling.*" Miss Evelyn beamed at Sydney. "You come by the Iron Horse sometime soon and see me, okay? Do you like ice cream?"

"Yes, ma'am."

"Oh, doesn't she have lovely manners!" Miss Evelyn wiggled the pom-pom over Sydney's head like a wand, making Sydney hunch her shoulders in a cute giggle. "I think Uncle Digger and I have a special treat with your name on it."

"Thank you, Miss Evelyn," Lana said, touched by more than the gesture to Sydney. It felt good to be greeted as an old friend. Even if she wasn't one.

Miss Evelyn winked. "You come see me, too. We'll catch up."

A male voice came over the PA then to make announcements, and Miss Evelyn shook her pom-pom again and yelled, "Go Warriors!"

Smiling, feeling positive and not really caring that others around them in the crowded stands had been watching with interest, she nodded and started the climb toward a spot in the third row where Davis and his kids had already settled with Jack.

Davis patted the space he'd saved. "Sit fast before someone grabs it."

A tap on the shoulder turned her around. She recognized the dark-skinned man immediately. "Creed Carter. Hello."

"I thought that was you, Lana. How's it going? When are we going to hear you on the radio?"

She figured she'd hear that question for a long time. "Never, I'm afraid. Nashville didn't work out."

"Their loss. Our gain." Rather than pursue the topic, he motioned to the woman and child beside him. "This is my wife, Haley, and our baby, Rose. Haley, meet Lana Ross. We attended high school together."

Easy as that, he introduced them. No references to her wilder side or any crazy stories from her past.

The two women exchanged greetings. Haley had an artsy, natural quality about her that Lana found interesting. Fair-skinned with no makeup, she wore her shoulder-length auburn hair loose with a silk flower pinned above one ear. The bouncy, apple-cheeked baby had olive skin and dark hair like her father with bright button eyes and a happy, alert expression. Lana liked them both instantly.

With an inward sigh of relief, Lana thought things were going very well. Maybe she'd misjudged Whisper Falls. Sure, a few people whispered and stared, but maybe the adjustment wouldn't be so difficult after all.

The PA announcer asked everyone to stand for the national anthem and the capacity crowd grew quiet. Ball caps were ripped from heads and held over hearts. Mothers shushed their children. Football players stood at attention, sweat already gleaming on their young faces.

Lana was always amazed at how, even in a large stadium, silence could shimmer through the autumn air like a cold front while the band played the dignified, rousing tune. As the music reached the crescendo, cymbals crashed. Goose bumps prickled Lana's arms. An undeniable longing to sing rose up to clog her throat. A longing she would never again see fulfilled.

By the end of the first quarter, Davis had memorized the main players and numbers, and he suspected Lana had too—at least on the Warriors' team. She was smart, jotting notes in her spiral notebook, noting specific plays, asking astute questions about the game as she scribbled away.

She was also smart enough to know she had drawn plenty of stares and whispers since their arrival. Only a handful of people had greeted her but plenty had stared outright as they'd passed. Maybe he was being oversensitive after Jenny's remarks, but their behavior put him on the defensive. He thought they were being ridiculous. Time passed. People changed. Get over it. Maybe they were just curious about the newcomer, the woman who'd gone to Nashville to be a star and come home again with a daughter.

Whichever, he was glad they'd sat together. She'd made him and Jack laugh more than once and she was kind to his kids—Nathan, in particular, who repeatedly found reasons to stand in front of her and ask eight-year-old questions. She'd been patient to the extreme even when she'd missed seeing a quarterback sack and worse, when she'd missed a touchdown.

"Nathan," he said. "Sit next to me." He patted the side opposite Lana.

"That's okay, Daddy. I don't mind standing up."

"You're blocking Lana's view."

Nathan flashed worried eyes to Lana. "I am?"

Lana opened her mouth to speak but appeared to reconsider before saying, "I like your company, Nathan."

"See, Daddy? Lana likes me. She's pretty. Don't you think she's pretty?"

He was not touching that with a ten-foot-pole. Instead, Davis leaned in to Lana's ear and whispered, "Pushover."

She shrugged and pulled Nathan close to her knees.

Just then, the Warriors scored on a long breakaway run and the crowd erupted. Davis leaped to his feet, anxious to get his son's attachment to Lana out of his head. This was a football game, not a date.

When the buzzer announced halftime, the score was tied fourteen to fourteen. Lana made a note in her book before turning to him. "I owe you some chili and popcorn."

"Sounds good to me. My lunch is long gone."

"You didn't have dinner?"

"Not yet." He grinned down at her, feeling that unwanted tug of attraction. He had a feeling there was a lot more to Lana Ross than her rough teenage years and a stab at stardom. The troubling thing was, he liked being around her. He liked *her*. Was he out of his mind?

Nathan pushed against Davis's legs, drawing his attention away from Lana and the uncomfortable thoughts. "I'm cold, Daddy."

"Want some chili?" Lana asked, smiling down at his son, who had taken Sydney's spot at Lana's side when Sydney had moved down to sit next to Paige.

"Uh-uh. Can I have hot cocoa instead?" Nathan asked, hopefully.

"Yes, you can. But aren't you hungry?"

"I don't like chili."

"Maybe a hot dog?"

"Yeah!"

Davis stooped to pull up the boy's hood and tie it under his chin. His cheeks and nose had reddened. "There's a blanket in the truck if you need it."

"I'm not a baby, Dad. I'll be okay after Lana gets me a hot dog and some cocoa." Nathan beamed a gap-toothed grin at the object of his affections, his gray eyes shining under the stadium lights. "You sure look pretty, Lana. Are you having fun with my daddy?"

Lana exchanged an amused glance with Davis.

"Yes, I'm having a good time, Nathan. Your dad is a great spotter."

Nathan was right. Lana looked pretty in her skinny jeans tucked into high-heeled boots and wearing a fitted leather jacket over a white shirt, her dark hair swooped up on the sides and large hoops dangling in her ears. A cheetah print scarf cozied up against her throat.

"Yeah. He's the best daddy in the whole world. He's nice, too. Don't you think my daddy's nice?"

"Very nice," Lana obliged, tapping Nathan's up-turned chin with a fingertip.

Exasperating as it was, the boy's innocent match-making touched Davis down deep. Nathan didn't remember Cheryl. But he apparently longed for a brown-haired woman in his life, for a mother. As hard as he'd tried to be everything to his kids, Davis couldn't be a mother.

The group tromped down the wooden stadium bleachers through the crowd of spectators and across the end zone to the concession area. The line was long and the smell of nachos and popcorn strong enough to make them worth the wait.

"I gotta *go,* Daddy," Nathan said, hopping up and down in the classic stance.

"I'll hold our place in line with the girls," Lana said to Davis, "if you want to go with Nathan."

"Thanks." Taking Nathan's hand, Davis made his way toward the men's room.

He returned to find the females still in line, talking to Retta Jeffers, a woman from their high school days. From the stiff set of Lana's shoulders and the red blotches on her cheeks, the conversation wasn't particularly comfortable. As he approached, Retta took her husband's arm and walked away.

Unsure of what to say, Davis looked at Lana in question. She met his gaze and then looked away.

Something was not right.

"You okay? You seem upset."

"Fine."

"That lady wasn't nice to Lana, Daddy."

"How so?"

Lana put a hand on Paige's shoulders. "It's all right, Paige. Let's not talk about it anymore. We won't let her spoil our fun, okay?"

Paige looked from Lana to Davis. The longing to tattle was clear and Davis wanted to know what Retta had done, but he didn't push.

"Okay." Paige took a deep breath. "But I'm gonna pray for that lady."

Lana's closed face softened. She pulled his little girl close to her side in a gentle hug. "That's exactly the right thing to do, Paige. Thank you."

Lana's response encouraged Davis. Though he was a Christian, he didn't push his faith on other people and he normally didn't pry into their business. But he wanted to know if the woman up the street was a good influence on his children. Not that being a Christian made her perfect. Lord knows he had his share of negatives. But if she was a woman of faith, perhaps Jenny would stop nagging him. Or not. Jenny had her own way of looking at things.

The line shifted and they moved closer to the concession counter. With an effort at keeping the conversation flowing, he said, "Do we have our orders ready? This place is a madhouse tonight."

"We do." She patted her notebook. "Jotted them down so I wouldn't forget. Chili, popcorn and Coke for you, right?"

"Right." He pulled his wallet from his pocket.

Lana pushed his arm away. "My treat, remember?"

"Hey, I was joking. I never let a lady pay."

"I invited you. I pay."

After a bit of haggling, she agreed to let him pay for his children, but not the rest. She paid for his, as she'd promised. The idea felt a little awkward. Call him prideful, but he preferred to buy.

With a mountain of junk food and drinks in hand, they started back through the crowd to their seats. A Latin-themed halftime show was going on in a dazzling display of gold and blue. The uniformed marching band strutted around the empty field behind somersaulting cheerleaders and a flag-waving drill team.

Lana froze in the end zone. "Oh, my goodness, I should be getting pictures of the band!"

She juggled popcorn, coffee and the notebook, finally bending to place them on the ground while she snapped some photos. "I'm never going to be good at this reporter stuff."

She seemed genuinely upset and Davis had a feeling her distress had little to do with missed photos and a lot to do with Retta Jeffers.

"You want to tell me what happened earlier with Retta?" He knew she didn't but he was asking anyway.

"Not particularly."

"Will you?"

She slid the camera into her back pocket and retrieved her belongings from the grassy field. Steam rose from her coffee cup and a few kernels of popcorn fluttered to the ground like snow against the green grass.

"Let's just say she brought up some unpleasant things from our high school days. I was on her hate list."

"That's what I figured." He moved closer, bothered by her downcast eyes and tight mouth. "They should let it go. High school is ancient history."

"Yeah." She sighed and looked down, biting her lip. "But I can't blame someone else for the way I was."

"Hey." Hands full but wanting to comfort her, he nudged his shoulder against hers.

To his chagrin, she took a step away and said, "Better get back to our seats before the game resumes."

Lana's head hurt. After the encounter with Retta, she wanted to go home. A dozen people in the line had heard Retta's snide remarks and innuendoes about Lana and her sister. Worse, she'd insulted Davis, asking how Lana had gotten her hooks into the grieving widower.

She straightened her shoulders, determined not to let one hateful person push her out. She'd known this would happen, known she would encounter people who didn't like the person she'd been thirteen years ago. Even *she* didn't like the person she'd been in high school. She'd hurt some people, especially the girls, and she'd made her share of enemies.

Now, the last thing she wanted to do was cause gossip about a nice man like Davis Turner. So, she walked a step away, putting distance between them, protecting him and his adorable kids from her reputation.

The inner voice that said she wasn't good enough started talking. She'd worked hard to keep it quiet. Those kinds of thoughts had pushed her to drink, and she wasn't going back there again.

Swallowing hard, she prayed an inner prayer for strength and peace and walked past the now silent Davis.

Such a nice, nice man. What was he doing here with her?

On the way back to their seats, they encountered more familiar faces. Most expressions seemed curious but not malicious like Retta. Lana began to relax again, though her good mood had soured. She understood their curiosity. She'd told the town she was going to be a star. Naturally, they would wonder what had happened.

She stopped occasionally to field the Nashville questions, avoiding the dark side, and simply repeated the limited truth. Things had not worked out in Nashville the way she and Tess had hoped, but they'd learned a lot and met a few stars. The last always turned the conversation away from her and toward the handful of famous people she'd encountered.

When the football game resumed, she breathed a word of thanks. She could do this. She would do this. She had a job to do and, for Sydney's sake, she would not let Retta or the past take away this opportunity.

By the end of the third quarter, Lana was so focused on the game, her notes and the photos that her headache ebbed. As the players trotted off the field and the band struck up a fight song, Paige and Sydney required a trip to the ladies' room. Haley Carter, sitting behind them, asked to tag along, leaving the baby with Creed.

"How long have you and Creed been married?" Lana asked as they walked, jostling shoulders in the crowd, voices raised above the pounding drums and chanting cheerleaders.

"About a year."

Their baby was older than a year, but Lana was

certainly not one to comment on that. "Creed was always a good guy. You look happy. So does he."

"He's amazing. The best husband. The best dad. My best friend. Can you tell I adore the man?" Haley laughed softly, her face aglow with a love Lana could only imagine. "Did you know he has a scenic helicopter service?"

"I'm not surprised. He always wanted to fly. That's what I remember most about him."

Creed was also one of the guys too focused on his goals to hang out much with girls, especially girls like her. He'd treated her with respect...and plenty of distance. Except for when they'd been lab partners in biology.

Haley tossed her auburn hair behind the shoulder of her wrap-style coat. "Can you imagine Creed marrying a woman who is afraid of flying?"

"Seriously?"

"Seriously, and he loves me anyway." Haley pushed her hair back, nose wrinkling in amusement. "Which proves he's either a wonderful man or a little crazy. Probably both." They chuckled together before Haley continued. "Davis is a nice guy, too. We attend the same church. Have you been dating him long?"

Lana stopped so fast Sydney slammed into the back of her. "We're not together."

"Oh?"

"I mean, we're together. For tonight. He's my spotter. The football players. For the newspaper.

I work there." She was rambling. She clapped her lips shut.

Haley placed a hand on her arm. Her fingers were short-nailed and stained with paint. Lana found the look comfortable. Haley was real. "I assumed and shouldn't have. Never mind. I'm sorry."

"Don't be sorry." She didn't want to lose this budding friendship. "He's only my neighbor. Really."

Davis Turner was so far out of her league, she'd never considered that people might think they were together, as in a date. Given his children's charming matchmaking attempts, she should have. Well, let them assume. As long as it didn't hurt Davis or his kids.

She was *so* not the right kind of woman for Davis. Even if she wanted to be.

Chapter Seven

At 4:00 a.m. Lana leaned her forehead on the laptop keyboard and closed her eyes for a tenth of a second. Exhausted but too worried about the newspaper article to do anything but work, she'd written and rewritten until her eyes were dry and gritty.

"This is harder than it looks," she murmured to the quiet. "A lot harder."

After reading dozens of online posts about writing a newspaper article, she'd hoped to get her thoughts organized. At this late hour, they'd become jumbled and skewed. She had names, positions and plays but what did she do with them? And how did she decide which were most important?

"Aunt Lana?"

She jerked her head up, stunned not to have heard Sydney's footsteps on the wooden stairs. "What are you doing up?"

The little girl's hair was a tousled, curly mess, her aqua eyes droopy with sleep. One leg of her pink princess pajamas rolled back on itself to display a shin bruised from a fall against the school merry-go-round. "I missed you."

Lana's heart constricted with a love she could never put into words, no matter how hard she tried.

Both she and Sydney had been sleeping in Sydney's pink-and-purple room, the first to be redone while working on the rest of the house. For now, Lana knew the arrangement was a comfort to her niece. The old house's squeaks and groans would take some getting used to.

"I'm still working."

Sydney rubbed at her eyes and yawned. "Do you know what time it is?"

The adult question made Lana smile, though her mouth felt too weary to move more than a fraction. "Too late to be working, huh?"

"Will you come to bed now?"

Lana stared at the computer for two beats, sighed and hit Save before closing the lid. "I'll get up early."

Sydney's giggle was drowsy. "You already did."

Wearily, Lana traipsed up the stairs behind her niece. Maybe things would look better after a couple of hours of sleep. They had to. The article was due before ten.

Someone was breaking down the door.

Lana shot up in bed, heart banging wildly against

her rib cage. Next to her, Sydney stirred and mumbled something unintelligible but didn't wake.

Lana tossed back the covers, grabbed her trusty baseball bat and tiptoed down the stairs, the wood cold on the bottoms of her warm feet.

The pounding came again, along with voices.

She paused on the bottom step to listen. A man's voice. Then something scraped across the porch. And a dog barked.

She frowned, more curious now than afraid. A burglar didn't bring his dog.

At the door, she peered through the tall glass side pane and spotted three familiar figures. One of them wore a tool belt.

Lana blew out a relieved sigh and yanked the door open. The sun nearly blinded her. "You're up early."

Davis Turner stood on a ladder repairing her gutters. On the porch Paige played tug-of-war with a small, shaggy white dog and a knotted doggy rope.

Davis grinned down from his high perch. He looked really good this morning. Too good. "I said I'd be here by eight. Remember?"

Shock made her jerk. "Is it after eight?"

He glanced at his watch. "Eight-thirty-five. I take it we woke you up? You gonna hit me with that thing?"

Lana looked down at the bat in her hand. "I forgot."

"I can see that. Sorry. Want us to leave?"

She propped the bat against the wall of the house, trying to get the cobwebs out of her head. She must look a sight. Barefooted. Ancient gray sleep sweats. Hair everywhere.

"What time did you say it is?"

"Eight-thirty-seven now." He backed down the ladder. "Want me to make some coffee?"

Dismay filled her. "I was supposed to turn in the article by ten."

"You've got time."

"No, I don't. It's not finished." But she was. Finished. Kaput. Out of a job.

"How long could it take to write up a football game?"

She glared at him and reconsidered the ball bat. "You have no idea what you're talking about."

He dropped his hammer and fittings into a toolbox. The metallic clatter gave her a headache. The glare gave her a headache. Her utter failure gave her a headache.

"Ooooh," she groaned, backing into the house. She was awake now, fully aware of her disheveled state, the unfinished article and one very appealing neighbor standing in her living area in a tool belt and a gray plaid shirt.

"Have you started on it?"

"Worked until four this morning but it still doesn't seem right."

"Maybe I can help?" he asked, sounding every

bit as uncertain as she felt. "I'm not a writer but I know football."

Desperate as she was, that was enough. "Would you?"

"Go," he said, flicking his hand. "Get your computer or whatever. Let me see what you've got. I'll make coffee."

She was up the stairs, dressed and had her hair yanked back in a headband in minutes. Sydney awakened and upon hearing that Paige and Nathan and a dog were on the porch, threw her clothes on and rushed outside.

Laptop in hand, Lana made her way into the kitchen, bolstered by the scent of strong coffee.

"There you go. No sugar. A spoon of milk. Hot and strong." Davis slid a faded Snoopy mug onto the chipped and equally faded counter before pouring himself a cup.

Lana blinked down at the mug in puzzlement. He knew how she liked coffee? "Remind me to pay you a bonus."

As she settled on the stool and sipped, Davis joined her. He smelled good, like a fresh shower, a little outdoors and just the right amount of woodsy sandalwood aftershave. Having once done a three-week stint as a sales clerk at a Dillard's cosmetic counter, she could probably name his cologne. Not designer but not cheap either. Something she liked. A lot.

He reached for the laptop, turning the screen in

his direction. A nice waft of the fragrance came with him. "Let me see."

She blew across the top of her coffee, waiting while he did a quick read-through. Once he said, "hmm," which told her nothing. She took a sip of the brew. Stronger than she made it but not bad.

Finished reading, he tilted away from the computer in a contemplative mood.

"What do you think?"

"Not terrible. You're a good writer."

"But?"

"Some of the football language is missing and a few places you could summarize the number of tackles, the run and pass yards, other stats for each of the top players of the game instead of that long list of everyone."

"Oh. Makes sense." She pulled the screen back to her and set her coffee mug aside. As she read through, she saw what he meant and made changes here and there, trimming the extraneous words and getting to the point.

For the next forty-five minutes, they talked last night's game and Lana rewrote. She was distracted at times, especially when Davis leaned in close to the small screen so they were practically cheek to cheek and that tantalizing scent she couldn't quite name tickled her nose. But at fifteen minutes until ten, she had no choice other than to send the document to Joshua Kendle's email address and hope it was good enough.

Breath held, she hesitated two beats and then hit Send.

"Do you think Joshua will like it?" she asked, rubbing the back of her neck, stiff now from tension and bending over the screen.

"He's an easygoing guy. He'll edit it for you."

That wasn't too encouraging. "I'll do better next time."

"The library might have some journalism books."

"That's a good idea. Online articles are helpful, but they're all mostly the same. After who, what, where and when, I'm pretty much lost."

He poured himself another cup of coffee and straddled a chair, arms folded across the back, mug cupped in both hands. "Do you remember Meg Banning?"

"No, I don't think so. Should I?"

"Probably not. She's in charge of the library."

Lana snorted. "A place I once avoided like the flu. No wonder I don't remember her."

"Nice woman. She'll help you out."

Lana angled her chair in his direction and then wished she hadn't. Having him in her space was… bothersome. "I take it you're a big reader?"

"I've been known to pick up a James Patterson novel, but the kids are the main reason I go to the library. Meg is great with kids. She does a reading program and a lot of other activities, especially in the summer, and Paige is a certified bookworm."

He flashed that wide-open smile that told of his affection for his daughter.

"And Nathan?"

"Nathan likes the cookies Miss Banning hands out during story hour."

A smile bloomed inside Lana and spread from her chest to her lips. "He's the cutest little boy, Davis. Such a charmer."

"Don't let him hear you say that. He's already half in love with you."

Lana squelched the uncomfortable wish poking at the back of her mind and came up with a joke of her own. "There is no accounting for taste but he's young. He'll learn."

"Hey! What is that supposed to mean?"

Lana felt the heat rush over face. "Nothing. A joke."

Davis *had* to know exactly what she meant. He'd heard the gossip, most of which was true, at least back then.

"You're still bothered by whatever Retta Jenner said last night, aren't you?" He took her coffee cup and refilled it. As he set the cup in front of her, he placed a hand on her shoulder.

Comfort. Friendship. Mr. Nicest-guy-on-the-planet doing what came naturally.

Don't read anything into it.

She shrugged him off. "A little, I suppose. People in a small town have long memories, Davis. I don't care about me. But I want them to give Sydney a chance. She's a great kid with the sweetest little spirit."

"How's she adjusting to the new school?"

"She likes her teacher but school is hard for her." She didn't relate the reasons for Sydney's struggles. She took the blame for the problem. If she'd been more stable, more unselfish, more sober, Sydney wouldn't have missed out on important learning. "Do you know if Miss Banning tutors in reading? Sydney could use some help."

"I can't say for sure, but you should ask. If she doesn't, she'll know someone."

At that moment, her cell phone chimed with a text. One glance at the message and her heart fell.

Her editor, Joshua Kendle, wanted to see her.

Davis hoisted one end of the claw-foot tub while the middle-aged buyer hoisted the other. "Cast iron weighs a ton."

"No lie, but my wife has wanted one of these things ever since we started building the new house." The bulky man's face darkened with effort. "Even if it costs me a visit to the chiropractor, it will be worth the money to see her expression on Christmas morning."

"Great Christmas gift idea."

"That's what I thought. I hope her mom doesn't let the secret slip. She's hiding the tub in her garage until then."

"Sorry you have to hold on to it so long but I'm

hoping to get as much of Lana's major work done as possible before the holidays. I need this out of the way."

"No problem, man. You're still on schedule to finish my tile work by Christmas, aren't you?"

"Plan on it."

The truth was, Davis was snowed under with work and adding Lana's to the list was overload, but he couldn't seem to say no. She had asked him to recommend subs, but why should he when he could pop up the street a few hours at a time and do the work for half the price? Lana didn't seem to be rolling in extra money so why not help out where he could? Being neighborly and all. He couldn't wait to see her amazement when he told her how much money he'd gotten for the old tub.

As he and the buyer started down the narrow hall, bumping walls and straining, Lana suddenly appeared in the opening. "Guys! Wait a minute. Let me help."

An hour ago, she had lit out of here a bundle of nerves. She was so worried about losing her job that he'd started worrying, too. She'd been on his mind for the entire time she'd been gone to the newspaper office, but from her behavior now the meeting must have gone all right.

"We've got it." Besides, what good could she do? She probably didn't weigh a buck twenty.

"Let me add my muscle."

Before he could laugh, she grabbed onto the

side next to Davis and lifted. Davis felt the shift in weight instantly and, impressed with the strength in such a small woman, was glad he'd had the good sense to keep his mouth shut.

"You balance," he said, admiring her effort. "I'll work the dolly."

With plenty of grunts and maneuvering they managed to get the old tub out of the house and loaded into the back of Ted's truck.

After Ted drove off, Lana opened the folded check and gasped. "Davis! He paid *this much* for that old tub and the fittings?"

Davis couldn't stop the smile that pulled at his mouth. "Happy?"

She turned those sparkling blue eyes on him at full wattage. "I can't believe it. This is enough to buy all new bathroom fixtures with a little money left over for Christmas."

Just as he'd imagined, she was thrilled. Beyond happy. Impressed.

Davis resisted the most powerful urge to toss an arm over her shoulders and hug her against his side. Last night's football game coupled with this morning's session at the computer must have rattled his brain. Not the game or the article exactly. The woman.

He shrugged, pretending a nonchalance he didn't feel. "Sydney needs to have an extra good Christmas this year. Moving to a new place is tough on kids."

Lana pocketed the check as she bumped his

shoulder with hers, teasing. "How would you know? You've lived in the same town all your life."

Davis liked when she teased. The meeting with Joshua Kendle must have gone really well.

He thought she looked great in a red sweater thing that came to her thighs and a pair of dark navy jeans tucked into her boots, her mink hair shining around her shoulders and her eyes happy. She was standing incredibly close, there in her front yard on that cloudy, gray November morning. A chill was in the air. Winter was breathing down their necks.

He gave in to the urge and dropped a casual arm over her shoulders. He felt her stiffen, just for a second, and then relax. But the reaction was enough to make him remove his arm. That was the second time today she'd pushed him away.

Get a clue, Turner.

"Where are the kids?" She stared around as if she'd lost them.

"Out in the backyard chasing Ruffles. Or being chased."

"Your poor dog must be worn out."

"Don't worry about Ruffles. He's in his element. Kids and more kids." Davis started up the steps. "Thanks for letting us bring him over."

Lana followed, hands stuck in her back pockets. "Sydney wants a dog so badly. It's nice of your kids to share Ruffles."

"Puppies make good Christmas presents. Cheap and easy. Adopt one from the pound."

She paused on the steps, head tilted. "Is that where you found Ruffles?"

"Yep. She was this bundle of white, matted fur, probably the ugliest little dog in the place." He cupped his hands in a gesture indicating her size and shape. "Both my kids went directly to her. She curled up in Paige's lap with this kind of sad, beleaguered sigh, and that was that. Puppy love at first sight."

"What a great story. I've never had a dog."

"Seriously?" He stopped. "You've never owned a dog? Don't you like dogs?"

"Yes, of course, I like dogs. I always wanted one but my mother said she was allergic, and since then…" She shrugged. "A dog wouldn't have fit my lifestyle. We moved too much."

"You should get one. I'm sure I could find a couple of eager young volunteers to go with you to the pound."

He held the door open for her, trying not to enjoy the sway of her hair and the smell of her flowery perfume as she moved past him. They were doing construction work. Dirty, nasty construction. Ripping out the old. Loading trash. Cleaning. Granted she hadn't helped all that much, but still, she smelled better than a flower garden. Looked better, too.

"I don't know," she said. "What if something happens and I have to move again?"

He paused in the living room to stare at her. "Why would you have to move again?"

She shrugged. "You never know how things will work out."

He wished he didn't understand her concerns but he did. Last night while she'd taken the girls to the ladies' room, his sister had made a point to corner him. As he'd expected, Jenny had been none too happy to see him sitting by Lana Ross. In fact, she'd insinuated he was damaging his children, subjecting himself and the entire Turner family to unnecessary gossip. Regardless of his plea that he was only helping out as spotter, Jenny had pleaded with him not to associate with Lana for the sake of his kids.

Yet, here he was. His kids were having a grand time, safe and sound. So was he. He felt good about helping Lana get the old house in shape. And yes, he liked her as a person. She wasn't the tough girl of old, though a thread of strength ran through her, a determination that, even if he didn't quite understand, he could admire. He didn't know where she'd been or what she'd been doing all these years, but Lana Ross was no longer a troubled teenager.

Yet, if his sister, a good woman who gave to charities and headed the benevolence committee at church couldn't see past Lana's youthful indiscretions, how would the rest of Whisper Falls treat her?

"You should make up your mind to stay, for Sydney's sake, no matter what. This is your home."

"For the most part I have made up my mind. Sydney's never really had permanence. I want that for her." Her boots tapped on worn and faded linoleum as they entered the kitchen.

"But you're holding back a reserve."

"I'm avoiding a puppy," she insisted with a pointed finger. "That's my only reserve. I don't have time for an animal right now." She opened the fridge and handed him a bottle of water. "I'll just borrow yours. Okay?"

"Deal. For now." He unscrewed the cap and swigged. "You gonna tell me what happened at the newspaper office?"

She took a water bottle for herself but didn't open it. The refrigerator shut with a soft whoosh of cold air. "He said the article was okay for a first-timer."

"That's it? That's the only reason he called you in?"

"He gave me some pointers and advice, showed me how he expected future articles to look, things like that. He was very kind." She widened her eyes in a grimace. "I was relieved not to get fired."

"See? Told you." He was ridiculously glad for her.

"Yeah, you did. Thanks for the boost of confidence and the help. I couldn't have done it without you."

He liked that more than he should.

"Speaking of getting fired," he said. "I'd better start that tile work or the boss will not be happy."

"She's a real slave driver." Her quick, easy smile warmed him. "A willing helper, too. Let's get to it."

He started to protest, to remind her that he could handle the job alone while she did something else. But the truth was he wanted her company. He wanted to know more about the woman his children wouldn't stop talking about.

Inside the old bathroom, a tedious job awaited. Over the years, home owners had layered linoleum over the original wood. Subsequent owners had added additional layers. He had removed all those layers before installing the backer board. He'd started on the open areas while awaiting the tub buyer's arrival and fortunately the bathroom was small.

Conversation was comfortable and mostly centered around the remodeling work, but Davis found Lana an easy person to talk to. She was witty, in a self-critical way that made him even more curious about what made her tick. Regardless, he liked her company.

Jenny would have an attack if she could read his mind.

But Jenny didn't run his life. She might be his sister and she might have his best interest at heart, but he was a grown man. He'd been making his own decisions for a long time. Granted, they all hadn't turned out well, but he was responsible.

His wife's untimely death flashed into memory. Prayer had absolved him of guilt, but he still wondered sometimes if he'd done the right thing. If Cheryl would still be alive…

He shoved the trowel under a chunk of ancient linoleum and pried it loose. On his knees, with Lana not three feet away also scraping at old, well-stuck glue, Davis let the rhythm of his work soothe his troubled thoughts.

The trio of children trooped to the entry and stayed a while to watch the adults sweat and work. Sydney, curly hair frizzing around her head like a halo, cradled Ruffles as she would a baby doll. The happy dog lay with eyes closed, head back, legs sticking straight up, being her usual rag-doll self. The little girl needed a puppy. He'd have to work on Lana about that.

"Whatcha doing, Daddy?" Nathan asked. He had dirt on his elbows and knees.

"Getting ready to lay out Lana's tile design."

"How long does that take?"

Davis sat back to look at the trio. "Why? Are you getting hungry?"

"A little," Paige said. "We were thinking maybe the five of us could go to the Iron Horse for hot dogs."

"Oh, you were, were you?" Davis shot an amused glance at Lana.

She was already shaking her head. "I don't think can make it today, kids. Too much work to do."

Davis scooted a box of tile into place and ripped open the cardboard top. Dust motes flew from the movement, sending the dank smell of old wood into his senses. "Tell you what? How about I order a pizza from the Pizza Pan?"

The children looked at each other and grinned. "Yes! Pizza!"

"You mind, Lana?" he asked.

Lana, sweeping bits of old vinyl and other trash into a dustpan, paused and leaned against the broom. "Sounds good to me. I skipped breakfast."

To prove the point, her stomach growled. The kids cracked up laughing.

"Okay, pizza it is." Davis took out his cell phone, a little embarrassed that the Pizza Pan was in his list of contacts. But what could he say? He was a single father. Pizza emergencies happened. Often.

"Daddy?" Nathan said again after the food and drink was ordered.

"What?" He removed several pieces of tile from the box and began arranging them in a pattern in one corner. Lana had chosen a marbled tan and sand with waves of off-white. The soothing, classic color had been a surprise. He'd expected something more flamboyant from someone who'd hobnobbed with famous entertainers.

"Can Sydney come to church with us tomorrow?"

Davis's head shot up. "Church? Sure, if Lana doesn't mind."

"Can Lana come, too?" Paige asked.

"If she wants to." He found Lana's eyes and held on.

She paused in her clean-up to say, "We need to find a church."

His heart jumped with gladness. Lana wanted to go to church. "Great. You can ride with us if you want."

Her smile did funny things to his stomach. Or was that hunger?

"Perfect. We'd love to, wouldn't we, Sydney?"

The little girl shifted Ruffles to her shoulder and nodded. Ruffles slouched forward with a sigh and settled her nose in Sydney's neck.

"And afterward," Paige announced with a clap, "we can all go out to Grandma's for Sunday dinner."

The unexpected comment not only surprised him, it put him on the spot. Davis didn't know what to say. Jenny would be there. Worse, he had no idea how Mom and Dad would react to him bringing any woman besides Cheryl to Sunday dinner, much less Lana Ross.

Little Miss Paige needed a good talking to.

He chanced a quick glance at Lana. She was busy loading a wheelbarrow nearly jammed full of trash and old flooring.

"Sydney and I have plans after church, Paige, but ~nk you for asking," Lana said as she shoved a ~iece of red vinyl into the wheelbarrow. Did he detect stiffness in the answer? Had she noticed his consternation?

"Rain check?" he asked. Clearing the way with his family was a necessity before he could invite Lana—or anyone—to a family gathering.

Lana glanced up. He put all the sincerity he could muster into his expression. He'd never wanted to be a hypocrite, one of those in-name-only Christians who talked a good talk but treated people shabbily.

"We'll see," she answered. He knew then, from the quiet hurt in her eyes, that she'd guessed. And he felt like a total jerk.

"I'll go empty the wheelbarrow," she said.

He had to give her credit. Other than short breaks, she'd stayed with him, working every bit as hard as he.

"Thanks." Troubled by his confusion and the voice of his sister in his head, he didn't watch Lana leave though he heard the rumble of the wheelbarrow.

The kids remained, observing with the curiosity of children and asking too many questions.

After a bit Davis sat back on his haunches and waved at the corner where he'd laid the first pieces of tile. He'd planned out a design pattern with diamond accents, already visible. Cutting each piece took extra time but Lana had especially liked the look in his portfolio of photos. "What do you think?"

The trio studied the tile as if they were experts, making him smile.

"Pretty, Daddy," Paige said. "You're the best tile putter-downer in the world."

"How about you, Sydney?" he asked. "This is your house. What do you think? Like it?"

Sydney's head bobbed. She wasn't a big talker but her expressive blue-green eyes said plenty. At the moment, they sparkled. "Yes."

"Ever had a fancy diamond pattern in your house before?"

Her small, oval face grew serious. "We never had a real house before."

The admission struck him in the heart. "Where did you live before moving here?"

He knew he was prying, but Lana was about as forthcoming as the Sphinx about her years away from Whisper Falls.

Sydney bunched narrow shoulders. "Sometimes in motels or other places. Sometimes in the car."

Whoa. What kind of other places? And what was a child doing living in a car?

Stomach rolling, Davis wanted to press for details but Lana chose that moment to return, wheelbarrow clattering against the hall floor.

As he looked up into Lana's pretty face, Jenny's voice echoed in his head. What kind of mother was Lana Ross?

Chapter Eight

Monday morning Lana dropped Sydney at school, and then stopped at the newspaper office, relieved to pick up another assignment. Afterward, with a renewed determination to learn more about this writing stuff, she drove straight to the Whisper Falls Public Library.

Unfamiliar with libraries in general, she was glad to see a row of computers, a desk manned by two women and more books than she'd known existed. Nothing weird or confusing. Surely, she could find help in here.

She approached a thirtyish redhead with stunning posture and a face that belonged on magazines.

"May I help you?" the gorgeous woman asked.

"I'm looking for Meg Banning."

Absolutely perfect teeth smiled at her across the desk. "I'm Meg. What can I do for you?"

This was Meg? No wonder Davis hung out at the library!

Somehow she managed to stutter around her surprise. True to reputation, Meg led her to a section of books and offered to order others through interlibrary loan.

"Do you have a library card with us?" Meg asked.

"Do I need one?" She hated feeling this stupid but libraries had never been on her list of hangouts.

"The application is short and easy."

"Will I be able to check out a book today?"

"Sure, though we limit you to two books per visit for the first three trial months." Meg led the way back to the desk where she withdrew an application from beneath the counter. "Here you go. Fill out all the contact information, add two references, preferably local, sign the bottom and you're good to go."

With a sinking feeling Lana worked her way through the easy part. Name, address, phone, employment. But at the reference lines she was stuck. Who in this town would vouch for her?

Finally, she scribbled two names.

"I moved here recently," she said as she handed the application back to Meg. "I'm not that acquainted yet but I think these two references will be okay."

Meg glanced at the names. Her beautiful face lit up. "You know Davis Turner?"

"He's my neighbor."

"Great guy and a terrific dad. You're lucky."

Was Meg the Beautiful interested in Davis? The notion gave Lana a funny feeling under her rib cage. Was Davis interested in Meg, too? Why should she be surprised that other women found him attractive? Any sensible woman would be thrilled to call Davis Turner her man.

Another patron approached the desk and Lana moved away to the stacks and shelves of books, shaking off the odd sensation. She wasn't jealous. She couldn't be. She and Davis were just friendly neighbors.

As she perused one volume Meg had recommended, several people moved past her, scanning titles. She shifted her position and, focused on the book, was paying no attention to the other browsers when a whispered conversation caught her ear. The speakers, hidden on the opposite side of the wall of books, were unknown.

"Did you see her at the football game? She was all over Davis Turner."

"Just like in high school. She probably slept her way around Nashville."

"I wonder what happened to her big singing career?"

"Singing? Is that what they call it these days?"

A giggle. "Retta, you're awful."

Lana's stomach churned. To her consternation, tears stung at the back of her eyelids. She spun away from the whispers and started down the aisle to escape the ugly gossip. One of the speakers was

Retta Jennings, who had never liked her, but the talk still hurt. She wanted to scream, "I've changed. I'm not that girl anymore." Instead, she pressed a hand to her mouth, closed her eyes and took several deep breaths through her nose, trying to recall her counselor's wise words, "You're a new creation in Christ. *You* know. *He* knows. But the rest of the world will need some time to catch up."

"Lana?"

She jumped at the sudden hand on her forearm. "Haley!"

Haley Carter, in a fleece-lined jean jacket and long corduroy jumper, stood in front of her, toddler in arms, compassion in her expression.

A hot flush of embarrassment rose on Lana's neck and spread over her face. "You heard?"

Haley nodded. "Don't let them get to you."

She let out a long breath. "I'm trying. No one seems to believe I've changed."

"No one?"

"Well…some don't."

"Only a few, Lana, and they don't matter. Don't let them matter." Haley shifted the baby to her hip. The pretty little girl grinned at Lana. "Want to go get some coffee and talk?"

Not that talking would help but she liked Haley and the Lord knew she could use a friend. "Let me check out this book first. Okay?"

"I have one, too." Haley hoisted a large volume of photographed artwork. Baby Rose grabbed the edge and tried to gnaw it. The young mother gently eased the book away.

They checked out at the desk and left the library, walking the few blocks down Easy Street to the Iron Horse Snack Shop. They took their time, letting Rose toddle along in her tiny baby steps. She was dressed warmly, a knit cap over her dark hair, and a soft fleece coat zipped to her chin. A beautiful child, Rose was happy, too, and clearly adored by her mother.

Lana stifled a regretful sigh. Haley was a blessed woman to have a child and a husband who loved her. In Lana's teen years, her thoughts about marriage and family had mostly been negative, impacted by her parents' constant battles. Today… well, today she didn't know. With her background, what worthwhile man would want her?

The day was cold and clear, the streets quiet. In the five-block swath that made up most of the town, they passed the Tress and Tan Salon where Cassie Blackwell pecked on the glass and waved a hairbrush. That simple act of friendliness made Lana feel better. Haley was right. Not everyone in Whisper Falls bore her ill feelings.

She waved back. "I met Cassie at church yesterday," she told Haley. "She and her brother and sister-in-law."

"The Blackwells are great people, not like some I could name."

"Yeah." The negative feeling returned.

"I know how you feel." Haley's voice was quiet as she stooped to lift Rose into her arms. Her skirt pooled around her boots.

"Oh, Haley, I don't think so. You're so sweet. I can't believe you ever did anything bad in your life that would make people hate you."

"I had an...unorthodox upbringing. Some people looked down their noses at me." Haley tossed her hair back and laughed. "And let's face it, I'm a little different. Creed calls it 'artistic' but those who don't love me have used terms such as 'weirdo' or 'flaky'. In fact, Creed called me Flaky Haley for a long time."

"He did not!" Lana couldn't help laughing.

"Yes, he did. I know what it's like to be...well, different. Kind of an outcast. Things have changed since I married Creed, but now I don't really care. I like who I am. Creed likes who I am. Most importantly, God likes me."

"My counselor keeps telling me that."

"Your counselor?"

Lana flinched. She hadn't intended to say that. The less anyone knew about her time in Nashville, the better chance Sydney would have for a normal life. "A mentor, really. Amber took me under her wing after I met Jesus and turned my life around."

"Things were bumpy in Nashville?"

"You could say so." And that's really all she wanted to say on the subject.

"Do you miss it? Your music, I mean?"

Like I'd miss my right arm. "That part of my life is behind me now. Sydney is my focus."

"Rose and Creed are my focus, too, Lana, but there's room for my art, as well. Having one doesn't mean I can't enjoy the other."

Haley had no idea what she was saying. Painting and sculpting were private art forms. Make a mistake and simply start over. Singing was make-or-break every single time she went on stage. Failure was one wrong note away.

Now, the only time she could sing was at night with only her guitar and her pen and pad for company. Alone, where no one would know the fraud she'd been.

But she was a long way from telling anyone what had happened to her singing career. A very long way.

Thankfully, they reached the Iron Horse, a snack shop connected to the historic train depot and museum run by Digger and Evelyn Parsons. Inside, the smell of cinnamon and apples filled the air, a result, she knew, of Miss Evelyn's almost-famous apple pie. A handful of small, square tables, unchanged in all these years, scattered around the small space while a counter with bar stools lined one end. A few customers sat here and there. Haley spoke to a couple of them, introducing Lana.

Along one wall of the room were an office door and an exit leading out to the train. The depot, which harkened back to the early days of the railroad, still displayed the rustic wood, antique green lanterns and other train paraphernalia.

Miss Evelyn came bustling toward them, her cheeks rosy in a round face. "Got some apple pie fresh from the oven."

Lana and Haley exchanged glances.

"Pie and coffee?" Haley asked.

"Sounds good. I'm chilled."

"Do you have a banana for Rose?" Haley said to Miss Evelyn.

"With a cup of milk?" the older woman asked.

Haley smiled. "Perfect."

"Coming right up." Miss Evelyn moved away in her characteristic rush, a sharp contrast to her amiable husband who never hurried. She returned with the order, lingering briefly to chat until another customer lifted his coffee cup.

"Awk. I'll be glad when Annalisa feels better. I don't know how we ever managed this shop without her. She runs the place now so I can do my work with the town council. When she's not here, I'm in a dither. With Thanksgiving just around the corner and the Christmas bazaar to plan, I really need her."

"Is Annalisa sick?" Haley asked. "She looked fine at church yesterday."

"Fine one minute, sick as a dog whenever she smells food cooking." Miss Evelyn pumped her eyebrows and grinned. "In a few months, she'll feel right as a summer rain."

With that pronouncement, she hurried away to the coffeemaker.

Haley's eyes widened. She peeled the skin from Rose's banana and broke the fruit into bite-size pieces. "The Blackwells are having a baby?"

A twinge of longing surprised Lana. "Sounds that way."

"I'm so happy for them. There is nothing in the world better than your own precious child." Haley bent to the high chair and kissed her baby on the forehead, receiving a banana-coated pat on the check in return. "Didn't you feel that way when Sydney was born?"

Lana dropped her gaze to the steaming apple pie. Guilt pressed at her conscience. Even though the deception was for Sydney's sake, she felt guilty for lying about the relationship, especially to someone like Haley who'd befriended her. "She was a wonderful baby."

She cut a bite of the pie and blew on it before tasting. Her answer wasn't a lie. It just wasn't the whole truth.

She chewed, expecting the pie to be delicious but it tasted like ashes on her tongue. Even a half-truth had a way of sucking the joy out of a situation.

"I never dreamed I would ever have a child of my own," Haley was saying.

"Why not?"

"I was afraid of getting too attached, of loving too much, of getting hurt."

"You? But you're such a great mother."

"It was only when I thought I was going to lose her that I woke up. Even though she wasn't mine by birth, I loved her. She was worth anything, even risking a broken heart."

"Rose isn't yours?"

Haley paused in wiping her daughter's face to give Lana a stern look. "Adopted means she's as much my daughter as Sydney is yours."

More so.

Again, the opportunity to tell the truth arose but the friendship was too new, so Lana kept quiet.

"I'm sorry. I didn't mean it that way."

"No offense taken. Creed is adopted, too, so he thinks adoption is the way to go. I'd like to be pregnant some day, but if it doesn't happen, I have the daughter I want, the child God intended me to have."

"And a pretty great husband, too."

"Absolutely." She pointed a fork at Lana. "So what gives with you and Davis Turner?"

"Nothing. I told you that at the game."

"I don't believe you. Neither does Creed. He said Davis couldn't take his eyes off you even when you and I went to the concession stand."

"Stop." Lana gave a short, embarrassed laugh. "He's a nice neighbor, taking pity on me. That's all."

Haley rolled her eyes. "Uh-huh. Whatever."

"Really, Haley. Even if I was interested, I wouldn't stand a chance. He is so out of my league."

And it hurt to admit the truth. Davis Turner occupied her time and her thoughts way more than was prudent.

"Is he dating anyone else?"

The question gave her pause. Hadn't she wondered the same thing? Davis had been working on her house nearly every evening after dinner. Some nights they ate together, usually a pizza delivered from the Pizza Pan, while planning strategies for the old house or talking about town events and football play-offs. If Whisper Falls won another game, they'd play for the state championship. Exciting stuff in a small town and especially for a stringer reporter who only made money when she wrote a story.

"Is he?" Haley pressed, hoisting her coffee cup.

"Not that I know of. But he's really busy with work and his kids. It doesn't mean he's interested in me!"

"But it doesn't mean he's not either."

Oh boy. Just what she needed. Another misguided matchmaker.

"Davis, you will *love* her. Tara is the sweetest girl ever. She's only been working for Chuck a short time, but he's mad about her."

After a hard, extra long day on the job, Davis was worn slick, grimy and ready to head home to the shower and a little time in front of a televised basketball game. The last thing he wanted was to be nagged about his single status. Again.

"Maybe Chuck should date her."

Jenny whacked Davis on the arm and growled like a bear. "Only if he has a death wish." She bared her teeth in mock anger. "My hubby is as faithful as that old dog we had when we were kids."

"Patches? Not flattering to compare your successful CPA husband to a Heinz 57 mutt." He gave up expecting to grab his kids and head home. Jenny was on a mission and he might as well sit down on her couch and endure her good intentions.

"Loyalty, Davis. Loyalty." She perched on the edge of the couch a couple of feet down from him, her back straight as an arrow, her dark blond hair fresh from the beauty parlor. "Now stop changing the subject. Tara Brewster is perfect for you. She's pretty and funny and smart as a whip. And she's new in town. Act now before some other smart man discovers her."

"I don't know if I'm ready for the whole dating thing, sis." Hadn't they had this conversation at least five times lately?

Jenny put her hand on his knee, her face filled with love and concern. She loved him, worried about him, even if he didn't want her to. "You know I loved Cheryl, but she's been gone a long time, Davis. You are young and good-looking—" When he flexed an arm, she pursed her lips and swatted him again. "Don't get the big head."

"Look, sis. I know you mean well, but I'd prefer to find my own dates."

"You aren't doing a very good job of it."

"I can't risk choosing wrong and messing up my kids."

"Which is exactly what you seem to be doing."

Her tone got his back up. "Are you talking about Lana?"

"I admire you for being a good neighbor. Even for bringing her to church. Lord knows, she needs it, but you can't let her get the wrong idea."

A cold feeling settled into his tired bones. Was this blind date Jenny's way of short-circuiting any interest he might have in Lana?

"What idea would that be?"

"You know what I mean."

Actually he didn't.

"Tara is more your type. And it would be a favor to me and Chuck if you'd go out with her. I know you're going to like her. You have so much in common."

He suppressed a sigh. Might as well listen and get it over with. "What makes you think so?"

"Tara's a widow. Car accident, I think."

He felt an instant, undesirable connection to the unknown Tara. "Any kids?"

"No. Which makes her perfect. Don't you see? She will adore Paige and Nathan."

At the mention of his children, a ridiculous, random thought penetrated Davis's mind. "What color is her hair?"

Jenny looked at him as if he was crazy. "What?"

"Remember Nathan's prayer?" A brown-haired mother. Preferably for Christmas.

"Oh, good cow." Jenny made a snorting noise. "Anyone can get brown hair if they want it. Tara's a blonde. A beautiful, green-eyed knockout. Nathan will fall in love with her. So will you."

Davis held up a hand. "Hold on now. It's only a date. I'm not marrying her, Jenny."

"So you'll go?" Jenny hopped up and hugged him. "Oh, I knew you would. You're the best brother. You won't be sorry, I promise."

Snared by his own words, he nodded, resigned. What would it hurt? If taking Chuck's new office assistant out for dinner would get his sister off his back for a while and Lana out of his head, he'd do it. Once.

"How did I get into this?" Davis muttered as he stood in front of his bathroom mirror and retied his tie for the fourth time. Anxious as a teenager dressing for the prom, he was not ready for this dating thing.

"Daddy?" Nathan appeared in the mirror behind him.

"What, buddy?"

"Can I go with you?"

"Not this time. You're spending the night with

Aunt Jenny and the twins. Remember?" He flipped one end of the blue striped tie over the other and poked the pointed fabric through the knot. The result was one tail shorter than the other. He pulled it apart again.

"I don't want to go to Aunt Jenny's. I want to go with you."

Davis dropped the ends of the tie, leaving them to dangle around his neck, and turned to crouch before his son. "What's the deal? You love spending the night with the twins."

"I don't like her."

"Jenny?"

"That girl. Paige says you're going on a date with a girl."

"That's right. I am. Her name is Tara. She seems very nice. I met her at Uncle Chuck's office this afternoon." Blonde, bubbly and sweet just like his sister had promised.

"What about Lana? She's real nice, too."

An arrow to the heart. But nice had different meanings to different people. As much as he liked Lana, some of the things he knew troubled him. Not for himself but for his children. He couldn't stop picturing little Sydney living in a car.

"Aunt Jenny is going to let you make Rice Krispie treats."

Nathan had a one-track mind. "Are you going to marry her?"

"We're going to dinner and a basketball game. That's all."

"I think I should go with you, Dad. I'm a good judge of character."

Davis hid a smile as he pulled his son into the *V* between his knees. "Not this time, buddy."

He hugged his boy close, enjoying the puppy-dog smell and tender love of his child. Paige had him wrapped around her finger. Nathan was wrapped around his heart. Both were too young to understand his dilemma. Being a single father, wanting to do the right things for his kids as well as address his needs as a man, was a difficult balance and part of the reason he'd avoided the dating game for so long.

Thanks a lot, Jenny.

"Dad?" Paige entered the room. Pixielike, with fairy-dusted freckles, she looked too serious this evening. "I'm worried about something."

"What's that, pumpkin?" He reached out to bring her into the family huddle.

"If you marry Uncle Chuck's assistant, what happens to Lana? Will that mean God doesn't answer prayers of little kids?"

Davis blew out a huffed breath. Good grief. This was getting crazy. "God always answers prayers, especially of little kids, Paige. But He doesn't always answer them the way we want."

"You mean Nathan might not get a brown-haired mom?"

"I can't answer that. I'm only going on a date. I'm not getting married."

Nathan raised his face so they were nose to nose. "Never?"

He shifted the children so that one sat on each raised knee, facing him. "Going on a date isn't the same as getting married, kids. Getting married means falling in love with someone very special, taking time to get to know her and then deciding if she's God's choice for our family. For all three of us. If I ever get married again, we'll all be getting married. Not just me."

Paige's gray eyes sought his. "You won't marry someone we don't like?"

"Not a chance."

"Promise?"

"Yes. I promise."

The children exchanged long looks before Nathan said, "Good. We like Lana."

Lana saw them come into the gymnasium. From her seat behind the clock keeper where she could take notes and see every play of the season opener, she'd spotted Davis and a pretty blonde the moment Davis had purchased tickets at the window box. He'd taken the woman's elbow, gentleman that he was, and guided her up into the stands where they'd sat down beside Mayor Rusty Fairchild, an Opie look-alike.

Davis had a date.

She tried to turn her attention to the pregame warm-up.

Sydney saw him too and leaned forward, gaze intent. "Davis is here but he's with a lady. Where are Paige and Nathan?"

"I have no idea. Sit up and don't stare." She pushed Sydney upright with a little more energy than usual.

She wanted to stare, too. Davis looked great, more dressed up than she'd ever seen him, as accustomed as she was to seeing him in work clothes covered with grouting mud or wall plaster. In a pale blue dress shirt with a darker blue striped tie and black slacks, he was killer handsome. When he smiled at the woman at his side, Lana expected the gym lights to dim in comparison.

The fluffy blonde woman was no slouch either. Dressed in a demure black dress with white pearls and trendy little heels, she was pretty as a picture. Davis couldn't seem to take his eyes off her. She was definitely his type. As sweet and wholesome-looking as a sugar cookie.

So, this was the woman Jenny had told her about at church, the woman Davis was dating. With all the flowery gushing of a mother, she'd discussed Tara Brewster, extolling her virtues, her Christian education, her classy lifestyle. With every gushy sentence, Lana had felt smaller and dirtier.

Now she got it. Jenny was warning her off, reminding her that Lana wasn't good enough for her brother. As if she didn't already know that.

With a heavy heart, she focused on her job and refused to look to the right again. The players, bouncing basketballs in staccato rhythm, moved off the floor, taking their places along the sidelines, to await the national anthem and their introduction.

"Can we get some popcorn?" Sydney asked.

"Not now." Though the buttery smell had her salivating, there was no way she was walking past Davis and his date to get to the concession stand.

The PA system squeaked and crackled. "Ladies and gentlemen, please stand for the singing of the national anthem."

The PA crackled again and Lana could both see and hear the conversation going on below her between the announcer and the high school principal. The crowd was standing, restless but waiting, but the music didn't start. She watched as a note was passed to the announcer. He cleared his throat.

"Bear with us a moment," he said. "Our singer has taken ill."

After a momentary pause, an unseen person shouted into the quiet. "Lana Ross is here. She can sing."

The blood in Lana's veins froze as people nearby began to turn and stare.

"Go on, Lana," the woman behind her urged with a smile. "Just like old times."

The woman had no way of knowing what she asked.

Lana shook her head but by now, the announcer had heard the comments and turned in her direction.

Her heart stuttered in her chest. She met his gaze, frowning as she mouthed, "No. Don't ask."

To her horror, the idea picked up momentum and the announcer said, "Some of you may remember hometown girl, Lana Ross, formerly of Nashville, Tennessee. How about it, Lana? Would you do the honor of singing our national anthem the way you used to?"

A sea of smiling, expectant faces stared at her. Her body went hot and then cold and then hot again. Her stomach rolled. Her knees and hands started to shake.

She shook her head vigorously. "No."

"Ah, come on, Lana. We remember your pretty voice."

"I don't sing anymore. I'm sorry."

He turned to the spectators. "Come on, folks. Give Lana a little encouragement."

The crowd started clapping. She stared around at the faces, some familiar, some not, but all expecting something she couldn't give.

Her chest tightened. Her heart pounded. The air grew thin. She couldn't breathe.

She leaped from the seat, climbing over laps and legs, stumbling blindly out of the stands, face aflame. Her body shook so hard she thought she might fall.

She hit the bathroom door with the palm of her hand and made it to the stall right in time to be sick.

Chapter Nine

Her light was still on.

Standing on his front porch, Davis slid the tie from his neck as he stared down the block at Lana's two-story. Something had happened tonight at the ball game that bothered him. He wasn't sure why she wouldn't sing the national anthem but her reaction had been over the top. Did she dislike Whisper Falls that much? Or as some had murmured, did she think she was too good to sing for such a small-time gig? Or was there another reason? Whatever, he was curious, bothered.

Now, as the cold, clear night closed around him and only the corner streetlight illuminated the neighborhood in dark shadows, he was very tempted to jog across the street and up the block. The kids were at Jenny's until tomorrow. Ruffles had gone with them. No reason to go inside the lonely house yet.

Before he could overthink the moment, Davis

stuffed the tie in his jacket pocket and jogged across the street to Lana's house. The neighbor's dog barked, a deep German shepherd *woof* intended to scare away prowlers.

Yellow light streamed out from a front window that opened into Lana's parlor. As he neared her porch, he thought he heard music, but the moment he knocked, the sound ceased. The porch light came on. He squinted, blinking as she opened the door.

"Davis?" Her throaty voice sent a shiver over him.

Sparkling conversationalist that he was, he said, "Hey."

She fumbled with the latch before pushing open the screen. "Come in."

"Is it too late?"

"Never."

He liked the sound of that. As he stepped inside, the warmth of the fireplace met him. She'd wisely had the chimney cleaned and serviced and now a snapping fire sent off a pleasant heat. A colorful, lopsided Thanksgiving turkey, similar to one Paige had made in art class, graced the mantel next to a cross and a photo of Sydney. Beside the hearth leaned the same acoustic guitar he'd noticed before.

"Nice."

She tilted her head to one side, lifting a shoulder. "A little early for a fire, maybe, but the heat felt good tonight."

She was dressed as she'd been at the ball game.

Skinny black pants, a lacy white, off-shoulder sweater thing draped over a red long-sleeved shirt. The only change was on her feet. Instead of her usual high-heeled boots, she wore fuzzy socks. The cozy sight made him smile a little. That was Lana. All country-singer trendy but real and comfortable to be with.

"You okay?" He shed his jacket without waiting to be asked.

"Great. Want some coffee?"

"Too late. I'd be up all night."

"The very reason I drink it." She smiled.

"In that case, why not live dangerously? The kids are spending the night with Jenny."

"Sydney's asleep, too. I usually work after she goes to bed. Sit. I'll get the coffee." She motioned toward the sheet-covered couch, but he followed her into the kitchen.

"I was worried about you."

At the counter, she glanced over one shoulder. "How so?"

"Tonight at the basketball game."

"Oh." She shook her head and turned back to the cabinets. "I'm fine."

Just that. She was fine. No explanation.

She loaded the coffeemaker and pushed On. "I'm working on the article about the basketball game. I think I'm starting to get the hang of this news-paper gig."

"Didn't you leave before the tip-off?"

"I didn't miss a second. Warriors went down 78 to 60."

Hmm. Interesting. She hadn't returned to the stands. He knew because he'd looked for her. He'd even been tempted to explore the lobby but with Tara at his side he couldn't. "Tough loss but the season's young."

She was standing with the upper cabinet open, her back to him, taking down cups and a container of powdered creamer. "How was your date?"

So she'd seen them. "A bust."

Lana head jerked toward him. "Really? She's so pretty."

"Can't argue that. Pretty, pleasant, good conversationalist."

By now, the coffee scented the room and warmed the end of his cold nose. Lana poured two cups. He reached around her and took one, brushing against her left arm. She looked up, met his gaze and went right on stirring creamer into her coffee. They were a whisper apart. In fact, he could feel the rise and fall of her breathing, detect the faint scent of mint on her breath and his heart seemed to swell in his chest.

"So what's the problem?" she asked.

Davis swallowed.

She wasn't you.

That's when the realization hit him. Jenny was right. He felt more than neighborly toward Lana Ross. In fact, if he didn't step away right now, he might kiss her. From the distant expression on her face, it was the last thing in the world she had on her mind.

He stepped back, taking his mug. "I don't think I'm ready."

She gave him a long, thoughtful look. "I understand."

Then, coffee in hand, she snapped off the light above the sink and headed back into the living room.

Lana settled at one end of the couch and curled her feet under her. Davis took the other end, cradling his coffee in both hands. He was comfortable here with Lana, in ways he hadn't been with Tara Brewster.

"Is she the first girl you've dated?" Lana asked, her husky voice sliding over his skin, warmer than the coffee.

He nodded. "Since Cheryl died, yes. Tara works for my brother-in-law."

"Jenny thought the two of you would be a perfect match."

Davis blinked, surprised that she'd known. "She told you?"

A momentary pause and then, "She might have mentioned something about it at church."

Jenny was talking to Lana about him? About his date? Why? As much as she disapproved of Lana why would his sister confide in her about anything? He had an idea and he didn't much like it.

"My sister doesn't run my life."

"That's good to know."

"Did she say something…?" He stopped. How did he ask if Jenny had insulted her without insinuating she had reason?

"I know Jenny doesn't like me, Davis. Don't worry about it. It's not as if you're interested in me."

But what if he was?

"It must be hard for you." She sipped the strong brew and watched him over the cup rim. "I mean, dating again after being settled and married."

"Really hard. Awkward. I loved my wife."

"She was a lucky woman."

"We had a good life."

"What happened? Or does it bother you to talk about her?"

"Not anymore. In fact, I wish people would talk about her more. My family is afraid of upsetting me or the kids."

"Paige has told me a lot about her."

"She has?" He'd had no idea his daughter was discussing something this important with the neighbor.

"She seemed to need that outlet. I hope you don't mind."

Did he? "I'm surprised. That's all."

"When I listen to Paige, to her wonderful common sense, her values, even her ideas about life and God, I know that Cheryl was a wonderful woman and a great mom."

Her compliment heartened him. "She was."

"Tell me about her."

Easy as that, she drew him out, listened, wanted to know, and he wanted to tell her. Everything.

"We met in college in Fayetteville in our freshmen year, first semester. Bam!" He whacked his chest with his fist. "Love at first sight. Married at Christmas, dropped out of school and came home to Whisper Falls. I went to work with Dad, using the skills he'd taught me since I was small. We never looked back. Cheryl worked at the bank until Nathan was born. By then, my business was going strong and she wanted to stay home with the kids. Really, that's all she ever wanted. Me, the kids, our life together as a family." He smiled, remembering the dark-haired woman who'd filled his life with love.

"I'm sorry. Really sorry for all you've lost." She unwound her legs from beneath her and shifted toward him. "Bad things shouldn't happen to such good people."

"I had a lot of questions, let me tell you. Questions that have no answers. That's the way this life is. If I believe God is in charge of the big things— and I do—I have to trust Him even in this."

"I admire that."

"Don't. I didn't get there overnight, but the bit about time being the great healer is true. Time and a couple of growing kids who needed me to be Daddy, not a grieving ball of mush lying across the bed." He huffed softly at the apt description, surprised he was telling her this.

"What happened? An accident?"

"No, but almost as sudden and every bit as unexpected. Sometimes I think if we'd done things differently, if I'd acted sooner, maybe she would still be here."

"You feel guilty?"

"Not guilty exactly." He shrugged, admitting the existence of that tiny niggle. "Maybe a little. Cheryl didn't like going to doctors. Of any kind. Once she had a toothache for a week before I could convince her to see a dentist. So when she got sick with what she considered the flu, we thought she'd be okay in a few days. She took over-the-counter medicines, stayed in bed. At her insistence I left the kids with Jenny, so they wouldn't get sick, too. But she didn't get better."

"She died of the flu?"

He shook his head, remembering the terrible moment when he'd known something much worse than flu infected his wife. "That last day, I'd taken off work at noon to come home. She scolded me, told me to stop worrying, and get back to work. It was the last time we ever spoke. When I arrived home that evening, she was unconscious." He drew in a ragged breath. "I couldn't wake her up."

"Oh, Davis, I can't imagine. You must have been scared out of your mind."

"I was." He dragged a hand down his face. "I

carried her to the car and drove like a madman to the clinic. Dr. Ron took one look at her and called Creed Carter to fly her to a hospital in Little Rock. She died en route. Cardiac arrest."

"But she was so young."

"She had some kind of heart defect we didn't even know about. Probably had it all her life."

The terror and shock followed by an ice-cold numbness came back to Davis. He'd been zombie-like for a while, with no emotions.

Lana set her mug on a scarred end table and scooted closer to him. "How awful."

"It was." He'd gone through the motions of life, of death, of a funeral. He'd accepted the flowers and sympathies, the fried chicken and prayers, feeling the love and compassion of a small town. The real grief struck later after everyone had gone back to their normal lives, but his life would never be the same again. "I know it's foolish to dwell on, but I can't help wondering now and then. What if I'd insisted she see a doctor, if I'd acted sooner when she didn't get better?"

Her hand closed over his. "God is in charge of things, even the big picture, right?" She gave his words back to him.

"Wise woman." Before he could think better of it, he put his arm around her and pulled her next to him. He knew he shouldn't have. It was a bad idea considering the late hour and the fact that they were completely alone without the worry of a kid inter-

ruption. Add the emotion of discussing Cheryl, the
dinner date that had made him feel more awkward
than anything and the nearness of this particular
woman. Touching her might not be a smart move.

She laid her head on his shoulder and sighed. His
pulse kicked up. This was nice, actually. Harmless
and nice. Sitting together on the couch with the fireplace snapping and the old house creaking around
them was a pleasant end to the evening. They were
simply neighbors having a conversation.

Then why did he have this overpowering desire
to kiss her?

He was going to kiss her.

Lana's heart thudded wildly against her rib cage,
a captive bird begging to be released.

Davis's fingertips, calloused and rough from
work, brushed her hair away from her cheek. The
rough tenderness sent a shiver through her body.
She wanted to reciprocate, to stroke his strong,
clean-shaven jaw, to snuggle closer.

They were alone. Sydney was asleep. The fireplace lulled with its golden glow and warm, crack-
ling flame. No one would know the nicest guy in
Whisper Falls had kissed the town's bad girl.

Was the man completely out of his mind? Was
she?

Reluctantly, she broke contact and scooted away,
thrusting about in her head for something to say.
Automatically, she went to the one thing that had al-

ways been her answer, her solace, her conversation when she had no words. She went to the fireside, picked up the guitar and strummed a quiet chord.

She dared a glance at Davis. He'd sat forward on the sofa, leaning toward her, puzzled.

She was puzzled, too. Puzzled by the sweet yearning to be something that she wasn't for his sake.

"You must wonder," she started, perching on the brick hearth, knees crossed to balance the instrument.

The caged bird beat harder, fluttering up to her throat. What would he think if she told him? Would he walk away and never return? And if he did, wouldn't that be the best thing for him and his beautiful little kids?

She searched his face, her chin high and cool as if she didn't know she'd rejected him. He watched her, eyes a stormy color.

"I wonder about a lot of things."

Lana thought she understood. He wondered why she'd hustled away, a woman like her with nothing left to lose. Certainly no reputation that mattered. He could stay here in her house all night and no one would be surprised that she'd allowed it. There might be a titter of conversation and Davis's reputation would be smirched but not hers. It was too late for her.

"That's not what I meant," she said.

He cocked his head, sandy brown eyebrows dipping to a *V.* "I think I'm lost."

So am I.

"At the ball game. I refused to sing tonight even though I've sung that song dozens of times." Her fingers found the strings and strummed again, restless, needing the comfort music could bring. "Do you want to know why?"

He shook his head. "I admit I was curious, but you have a right not to sing if you don't want to. It's your voice, your God-given talent. You can share it or not. Your choice."

"But you think I'm being selfish?" She could see the hint of accusation in his eyes, hear it in the slightly tense comments.

His gaze slid away from hers. "They shouldn't have pounced on you without asking first."

"What did they say?" She pressed, a glutton for punishment, wanting him to say something cruel so she wouldn't like him so much. The basketball crowd had complained. She was sure of it. This town disliked her and tonight she'd added to their long list of reasons. "Go on. I'm tough. You have to grow thick skin in the music business." Though she'd learned most of her toughness in Whisper Falls.

"Forget tonight. Like I said, your voice, your choice."

"I don't think I'm too good to sing in Whisper Falls, Davis, if that's what you think. And it's not about money. I've sung for nothing a lot more often than I've sung for pay." The whisper of a song pushed up in her throat. She let it loose, humming.

He rose from the sofa and came toward her. Her stomach fluttered. She fought down the quiver of emotion, one part of her wanting him closer, the other willing him to keep his distance.

"So, if singing tonight wasn't about money or prestige, what was the problem?" He stood too close, one hand on the brick surrounding the fireplace, his scent mixing with the wood smoke. He'd carried the night in with him and she could smell the stars and moon. Man and moon, a heady combination.

"Some things happened in Nashville. I lost my…" Telling him about the fear was easy. But what about the rest?

"Voice?"

"In a manner of speaking. I lost my confidence." Truth was, her confidence had been artificial, taken from a gin glass. But she couldn't tell him that.

"No way. Even your humming sounds incredible to me." He tugged at his pant leg and settled next to her on the hearth. "Rough honey. Isn't that what the *Music City News* said about your voice?"

She recalled the wild thrill of reading her name in the prestigious publication. "You saw that?"

His eyes twinkled into hers. "Everyone in Whisper Falls saw it. We thought you were on your way to the top. Small-town girl making it big."

Such a good man. Such a sweet, all-American face. Good to the soul.

"All I made was a mess," she admitted, the words tumbling out before she could stop them. But that was as much as she dared say. She couldn't bear for him to know the rest, the debauchery, the nights spent too drunk to remember. Before he could press for details, she said, "Somewhere along the way, I developed a powerful case of stage fright. I can't get in front of an audience anymore."

"Stage fright?" He blinked, head tilted as if he couldn't quite take in her admission. "That's why you wouldn't sing tonight? You were afraid?"

"More than afraid, Davis. Terrified. Panicked. I can't really even describe how bad it is." She found the strings again, this time finger-picking a soft tune she'd composed. "I get so scared I think I'm going to die. I can't breathe. My heart races out of my chest."

"Did you see a doctor?"

"Doctors cost money, and they can't cure what ails me."

"You're too good to let fear stand in the way."

"Thank you for that." The melody from her guitar floated in the space between them. A love song. "But I'm okay with letting it go. My career was over before it started."

"I don't believe you." He placed his hard fingers across hers, stopping the music. "God doesn't take back His gifts, and your gift is music. Look at you. The guitar is as much as a part of you as your beautiful hair."

He thought her hair was pretty? "I gave up singing, not music."

"Do you want to perform again?" He pulled his hand away, but hers remained on the strings, the feel of him vibrating through her skin.

"I—" She opened her mouth to deny the desire, but the words wouldn't come. She didn't want to sing the way she'd done before but oh, if she could sing unfettered by fear. If the songbird in her soul could fly free of its captivity. "Maybe," she ended.

He pulled her right hand from the guitar and into his, turning it palm up where he traced the line from thumb to pinky. Then he found the fingertip calluses, made deep by the frequent rub against the strings, and stroked them over and over. A tiny, raspy sound whispered from his skin to hers. A shiver, pure and lovely, ran along her arm.

"Do you believe in prayer?" he murmured.

"Absolutely." Prayer had literally saved her life. "Why?"

"The Bible says God has not given us the spirit of fear. He can take away that stage fright."

"You pray for me, then," she said.

"Count on it."

The thought of Davis calling out her name to God was a balm to her bruised spirit. God would listen to a good man like Davis.

They sat in silence for a bit, the fire warming

their backs and Davis's skin warming hers. She thought she should pull away but she couldn't. She'd always been weak.

After a few tender moments, he squeezed her fingers and turned her loose. "What about Tess? Did she stop singing too?"

"She still works the clubs." Some. When she's not too strung out to show up.

"You still write?"

He remembered that? "I tried selling some of my songs. No takers."

"Play one for me. You don't have to sing it. Just play."

"I don't mind singing at home." And even if she did, she'd play for him.

Her fingers coaxed a melody from the guitar, and this time she sang along, softly at first and then louder until the room filled with music.

"On wings of the wind, through the clouds and the rain, your love carries me, carries me."

She closed her eyes and let the music take her as it always could, letting the emotion flow. The words and the melody rose from somewhere deep inside, an underground cavern of diamonds and gold, hidden from the world but always there, rich and beautiful. Only when the music took her did she feel this way, as if she was elevated to another plane where nothing could hurt her.

She looked toward Davis. Was he feeling it too?

Yes, she thought he was, and she was mesmerized by his expression. Rapt. Impressed. Entertained.

The pleasure of sharing her music thickened in her chest. She hadn't felt that buzz of connection in a long time and it was good. Really good.

As the song ended and her voice faded away, the lilting melody hummed in the cozy quiet for several seconds.

Davis shook his head back and forth in a slow pendulum. "Wow."

Self-consciousness rushed in. "Does that mean, wow, it was good or wow, you're glad it's over?"

"That means, wow, I'd like to have a copy."

"Really?" Complimented, she pulled a sheet from a folder on the hearth. "Take it. I have more."

With a near reverence she found both touching and amusing, he accepted the simple sheet music. "You know this is amazing, don't you? *You're* amazing. Talented, gifted, whatever word you want to use. Not that I know a thing about writing music, but that was beautiful. And your voice is stunning. I don't understand why you'd be afraid to share it."

"You haven't been to Music City. I'm not too impressive there."

"Must be a really tough business or else you didn't meet the right people."

"You have no idea. Definitely not for the weak." Which she had been. She set her guitar against the wall and stood.

Davis followed her up where he stretched his

hands out toward the fireplace. He couldn't be cold but the heat was nice. She joined him, stretching out her hands as he had done.

He rolled his head her direction. "There's nothing weak about you, Lana."

"Oh, but I am. I was." She tossed her hair back, eyeing the ceiling with its fresh coat of paint. "That's why I'm here, in the house I swore I would never again lay eyes on. After I found Jesus, I had to make some changes for Sydney's sake as well as my own."

"Why did you hate this place so much?" He backed away from the fire, his cheeks rosy. "Why didn't you ever visit?"

She heard the accusation and knew he asked why she'd never visited her mother, why she'd missed the funeral attended only by an uncle and a few townspeople. She drew a deep breath and let it seep out, contemplating. What difference did it make if she told him?

"My family was about as dysfunctional as you can find. Or it seemed that way to me as a kid."

"I never knew that."

Why would he? They'd never hung out. "My dad kept up a good front but my mother was a nightmare. Looking back, I think she might have suffered from mental illness, but to a child, she was just plain mean. Tess and I stayed as far away from her as we could."

"Was she that bad?"

"Oh, yeah. That bad and worse. She did some things to us…." Her voice trailed off. "Mostly words but not always. She locked us in the cellar a couple of times overnight."

She tried to say it as if the abuse didn't matter, as if she wasn't bothered by her mother's cruelty but she knew she failed.

Davis, always Mr. Nice Guy, rubbed her back. She didn't read anything into it. He was a friend, offering comfort. "I'm sorry, Lana. Stuff like that shouldn't happen."

"We survived. It was just spooky and cold." She tossed her head and tried for bravado. "Gosh, I was mad at her."

So mad she hadn't gone home for three days. But mostly, she'd been heartsick that her own mother could hate her that much. And that her father could care so little that he'd leave and never even call. She'd found him once on the internet but hadn't made contact. What was the point?

"No wonder you didn't want to come back to this house."

"No, I didn't. That's for sure. But Sydney deserved more than I could give her on the road. At least here she has stability. This house may not be much, but it's ours." And Mama was gone. Lana felt guilty for being glad about that, but no matter how much she prayed, she was still glad.

"By next fall you won't recognize this place."

Which was exactly what she wanted. Wipe out

all the ugly memories and replace them with Sydney's laughter and her music. Even now, the living room felt cozy and friendly in a way that it had never been when she was young.

"If the money holds out."

"What about Sydney's father? Doesn't he help with expenses?"

The words were cold water in the face. She'd known he would ask, sooner or later. She also knew he wouldn't like the answer, but for Sydney's safety, the partial truth was all she was willing to give. Even if it meant he would walk away and never look back. For his sake, that's exactly what he should do. He and his children needed a woman like blonde Tara or one of Jenny's church friends, not a has-been, former drunk singer with the reputation of an alley cat.

"That isn't possible."

"Why not?"

A beat passed. A log fell and shot sparks. Neither of them moved.

Lana cleared her throat. Confident she was doing the right thing, she said, "I have no idea who Sydney's father is."

Davis lay awake a long time after he left Lana's house. Thoughts shot through his head like fiery arrows, sharp and burning. Tonight Lana had opened up to him as never before and he wasn't sure what to do with the information.

Her childhood had been horrible. He couldn't imagine a parent locking her child in the cellar, and he didn't doubt Patricia Ross had been abusive in other ways.

Despite her confession about Sydney's parentage, he was still attracted to her. He'd wanted to be with her, to kiss her, as badly afterward as before. Maybe more. Her strange mix of invincible warrior and vulnerability had touched him. She seemed so bravely alone, as if she expected him to pass judgment and kick her out.

Was the woman intentionally trying to push him away? Was that it?

He tossed onto his side, pummeled his pillow. She liked him. At least, he thought she did. Or was she using him, as Jenny had suggested, as a means to get her house remodeled?

No, that wasn't Lana. She'd never asked him for anything. Not once. He'd offered. She was the workaholic, stripping wood and scrubbing floors at all hours of the day and night.

No one had asked her to be kind to his kids either. She'd fluffed Paige's too-short hair for church, obviously feeling sorry for his little girl and her inept dad. Paige had been so proud of the curls and bows she'd pranced around like a princess.

A couple of nights ago, Lana sat on her couch next to Nathan and read the same story four times in a row. And time after time, she'd tolerated three children tearing wildly through her house or perching at her table for PB and J sandwiches. No, she wasn't trying to take advantage of his neighborly kindness.

The more he knew about Lana Ross, the less he understood. She was a contradiction, a mystery. A beautiful, gifted, complicated mystery. He was both muddled and mesmerized.

He recalled the power and beauty of her voice, and he wanted to hear it again. Just a hum from that smoky throat captivated him. So what had happened in Nashville to bring on stage fright so bad that she couldn't get on stage? She'd sung for him. Why not on a stage? She was twice the singer Tess was and yet, Tess was still in Nashville while she was here, writing articles for the *Gazette*.

The song she'd shared lingered in his mind even now. She should do something with it. Not that he knew anything about the music world. The lyrics and melody were a hauntingly beautiful combination, better than anything he'd heard on the radio in a while. Why hadn't it been published? Had she tried? Or was this one something new?

He flopped onto his back and stared up at the faint shadows on his ceiling. The house felt lonely. *He* was lonely. For more than his children.

Tossing the covers back, he padded to the window and pushed the curtains to one side. Curtains Cheryl had ordered from J.C. Penney years ago. Not unusual for him to think about those days when he and Lana had talked about Cheryl tonight. Another thing he liked about Lana Ross.

Fumbling in the dark, he found the lamp and snapped it on. Cheryl's photo sat on the bedside table where he'd placed it the day after she died.

"Hi," he said, as he'd done dozens of times over the years. Her brown eyes twinkled in response. At least in his imagination. "What am I doing up at this hour? Good question. You see, there's this neighbor. Yeah, a woman. Lana. What do you think about her? Should I run for the hills?" He chuckled quietly. "Oh, right, we live in the hills."

He studied the simple face of his first love, the crooked smile that they'd never had the money to get straightened, the sweeping length of brown hair he'd loved to touch.

That, of course, brought him back to Lana. Lana, of the brown hair.

Carrying the silver frame, he returned his gaze to the window and beyond. From this spot, he could see the old house down the street and across the way. Lana's light remained on. Probably working on her article for the *Gazette*. Or was she, like him, too restless to sleep? Too bothered by feelings neither of them seemed to want?

His breath fogged the cold pane. He placed his late wife's photo back on the table.

"I like her, Cheryl," he said, admitting the truth to the emptiness, but mostly to himself. "I'm not sure that's smart. She's carrying a lot of baggage, but there's something special about her, too. A lot special. She's a good person, a Christian, but she wasn't always. I know, I know." He puffed out a gusty breath. "It's the kids. I have to be sure. I have to do what's best for our kids."

Davis rubbed a hand down his T-shirt, kissed his fingertips and touched them to the photo.

Then he snapped off the light and climbed back into bed, no closer to answers than he'd been before.

Chapter Ten

Thanksgiving Day arrived cold and rainy, the skies weeping down the windowpanes of the Ross house. A blustery wind whipped the barren crepe myrtle trees against the needed-to-be-replaced siding.

Inside the house all was snug while the Macy's Thanksgiving Day Parade boomed from a nineteen-inch TV Lana had found at a garage sale. A vigorous marching band pounded out a cheerful, familiar rhythm. Surrounded by autumn color, a pair of talking heads blabbed over the music. Bundled against the cold, their breaths puffed white fog.

Lana stood over the gas range where warm moisture from boiling potatoes dampened her face. Sydney chopped lettuce for a salad. The ancient oven hadn't worked since Lana was fourteen, so she'd bought a precooked rotisserie chicken from the IGA for their main course. A turkey was too much for the two of them anyway.

Cooking wasn't Lana's game but as with her

newspaper job, she could read and she could learn. Sydney learned along with her, probably more natural in the kitchen than Lana would ever be. Store-bought chicken, canned gravy, packaged stuffing was as close as she could come to a traditional meal. At least she and Sydney were together.

Times like these she wished for a big, noisy family, especially for her niece. A mother who baked for days and a sister with the perfect recipe for sweet potato casserole and pecan pie. A dad to carve the turkey and maybe a few brothers to horse around and yell at televised football games. Sydney deserved better than one single aunt and an AWOL mother she barely knew.

"Can I smash the potatoes?" Sydney asked. She'd pulled her fuzzy hair into a ponytail and tied it with a purple ribbon, a match for her purple monkey sweatshirt. Loose beige curls corkscrewed along her hairline.

"Smash 'em, mash 'em, stomp 'em. Whatever works."

Sydney's aqua eyes laughed before her mouth did. Lana smacked a kiss on her forehead, then handed her Mama's metal potato masher, tossed some butter in the bowl and let Sydney pound away while she put the food on the table.

Today was the day they started their own holiday customs, something Sydney hadn't had heretofore. Lana had shared family traditions once, and the memories were some of her happiest. Daddy had made a fuss over the fine brown bird, which had made Mama smile. Usually by day's end, Mama found something to be angry about but the meal was usually peaceful, thanks to her father.

She wanted that for Sydney. Good memories, good times to block out the bad.

"Here you go, Miss Ross," she said, pulling the chair out for Sydney. "Please be seated for this luscious, marvelous Thanksgiving feast."

"Just like the Pilgrims," Sydney said as she minced into the seat like a pampered princess. "But who's going to hold your chair?"

Lana winked. "Good ol' me." She wiggled all ten fingers. "I'm so handy."

The silliness made Sydney giggle again. "This smells yummy."

"It should. I've slaved over that boxed stuffing for a full five minutes." She fanned her face and grinned, then took her place kitty-corner from the little girl who held her heart. "Would you like to ask the blessing?"

They bowed their heads and Lana listened, throat full, as Sydney prayed a litany of thank-yous and blessings.

Finally, she said, "And bless Paige and Nathan and their dad. I hope you give them a real good dinner like ours. Thank you for sending me a friend. And please take care of my mom. I hope she's okay. Amen."

Unexpected tears spurted behind Lana's eyelids. *Tess. Oh, Tess. Where are you?*

She pressed her fingertips hard into her eyelids to gain control. A small hand patted her arm.

"It's okay, Lana. God's taking care of my mom."

Most times she tried not to worry about her twin but she'd heard from her only once since the return to Whisper Falls. Tess had called, full of over-the-top excitement, an endless spiel of chatter and wild promises that told Lana immediately she was high. She'd tried to talk to her sister, urging her again to go to the mission for help. Tess had hung up on her.

"I wish I knew where she was." Lana scooped mashed potatoes onto her plate.

"You miss her," Sydney said, adultlike. "Maybe we can call some of her old friends?"

Most of Tess's friends had long since abandoned her but it was worth a try. Though Tess had never been much of a mother, she'd once been a good sister, and Lana *did* miss her. Terribly. "That's actually a very good idea, Sydney. After dinner, we'll give it a try. Now, do you want some of these fluffy, creamy, Sydney-awesome mashed potatoes or not?"

Sydney grinned and took the bowl. "And some of that Lana-awesome gravy and stuffing, too!"

They both laughed heartily at that comment, considering the foods were packaged.

"Paige said her grandma cooks everything in the universe for Thanksgiving dinner. They even have corn on the cob and chocolate pie."

"Wow. Wish I'd thought of that."

"It must be fun to have a grandma." Sydney drizzled brown gravy over the potatoes and stuffing as well as the chicken. A sea of gravy. "She lets Paige and Nathan and their cousins decorate cookies, and they play games with her, too. Did you ever have a grandma?"

"I did. My Grandmother Packard lived right here in Whisper Falls."

"Was she nice?"

"Really great. She sewed Tess and me matching dresses every year for Easter." Losing Grandma Packard at age nine had been a turning point in her young life and in her mother's, too. Mama's anger and moods had spun out of control once Grandma was gone.

"That's cool. I wish I had a grandma." Sydney's matter-of-fact comment hurt worse than if she'd whined in self-pity.

"Next time we're in Walmart, we'll buy you one." Lana pointed a hot roll. "Nine ninety-five plus tax."

Sydney put a hand over her full mouth and giggled. "Will you buy me a sister and brother too?"

"Tall order but why not? As long as they are on sale."

Smiling, feeling good, they continued their feast. The day was going great, better than she'd expected. *Thank you, Lord. Really. Thank you.*

"Lana?" Sydney said, putting down her roll and looking suddenly serious.

"Mmm-hmm," Lana managed to answer while chewing a succulent piece of chicken breast.

"You know what I'd really like to have more than anything?"

Lana swallowed and reached for her coffee cup. "More than a grandma or a brother or a sister?"

"Yes, even more than that."

A puppy, Lana was certain. She was going to have to give this pet thing more serious thought. "What?"

"A daddy. A real good daddy. Just like Davis."

The kids were bouncing off the walls.

Davis, his belly full, flopped into his recliner and pointed the remote. Mom had outdone herself this year. He couldn't think of a single Thanksgiving food she hadn't produced at some point during the rainy day. They'd stayed even longer than usual playing board games and snacking while the Cowboys and Lions battled on the gridiron.

He snagged Paige as she romped through with Nathan in hot pursuit. "Good day, huh, pumpkin?"

"Yep, except I felt bad for Charlie. He didn't even feel like eating Grandma's magic cookie bars."

Jenny's son, always frail, had seemed worse today. He'd slept most of the afternoon, worrying his parents.

"Me, too." He hugged his child, thankful for her robust health. "Aunt Jenny is taking him to the doctor in Little Rock tomorrow."

"I hope he's better. He said he was going to have to get an operation."

"That's true."

"I prayed for him."

Of course she did. That was Paige. Freckles and faith.

Nathan, who stood beside Davis's chair, head cocked as if he was listening, clearly wasn't. He said, "I'm hungry."

"Hungry?" Davis burst out laughing. "You can't be hungry."

Nathan pooched out his belly, rubbing the tiny mound beneath his camo T-shirt. "Can I have some pie?"

"Grandma sent home enough leftovers to last a week. Go for it."

Paige, still draped across Davis's lap like a blanket, patted Davis's neck. "Daddy, why doesn't Aunt Jenny like Lana and Sydney?"

Whoa. Where had that come from? He grasped Paige's hand and sat her up. "Did she say that?"

"She said Lana was a bad person and she might hurt us. I heard her tell Grandma."

Heat rose on the back of his neck. Where did Jenny get off saying such a thing? "Lana's *not* a bad person. Aunt Jenny's upset because Charlie's sick. She says things she doesn't mean."

"That's what Grandma said. She said you have to be careful about judging people. She said Lana might have problems we don't know about."

Thanks, Mom. "Grandma's right."

"Does Lana have problems, Daddy? She's really nice to me and Nathan. I'm sure she would never, ever do anything to hurt us. Never. We love her. I don't think she has problems. I think she's wonderful, like Mommy was."

"Everyone has problems, pumpkin. Lana is no different than Aunt Jenny or you or me."

Davis felt like a hypocrite, considering how he'd wrestled with Lana's admission about Sydney's father. How did a woman not know who fathered her child?

But all day today he'd thought about her. Not just today but every day. Even though he'd avoided her house all week, he thought about her. Missed her.

When they'd pulled into their driveway after the wonderful day at Mom's and Dad's, he'd noticed her car was home. His conscience had twinged then and it twinged now. Today was Thanksgiving, a family day, a day he and his children had basked in all the noise and pleasure that was family. Yet, he was fairly certain Lana and Sydney had spent the holiday alone.

He should have invited her to the Turner Thanksgiving madness, regardless of Jenny. He didn't appreciate the seed of gossip his sister had placed in his daughter's head. That was wrong, no matter how upset or how protective Jenny might be.

He popped his chair upright. "I have an idea.

Let's take one of Grandma's pies over to Lana and Sydney."

Ten minutes later, he and his kids stood on the Ross porch, each of them holding containers of food. The rain continued to drip like a leaky shower from a cold, slate sky.

Lana opened the door. As soon as she saw him, her smile bloomed. His stomach, full as it was, went south. He smiled back, staring long enough that Paige said, "Dad! It's cold out here."

Lana blushed a pretty pink and opened the door. They flooded inside, all talking at once. Sydney exclaimed over the pecan pie while Nathan hugged Lana's waist and told her she was pretty. She hugged him back and told him he was the handsomest little boy she'd ever seen. Then the trio of kids headed to the kitchen to eat pie as if they hadn't eaten all day long.

"How was your Thanksgiving?" Lana asked once the kids had disappeared.

"Great. The whole clan was there. Even my aunts and uncles from out of town." *Everyone I wanted to see except you.* "So how did the Rosses celebrate?"

"We made dinner together and watched a Christmas movie. The oven doesn't work so we had Oreos for dessert. And ice cream."

He laughed. "Works for me. Ice cream on top of pecan pie sounds pretty good."

"Want some?"

No. I want you. I want to hold you and smell your hair and touch your creamy-looking skin.

Davis shook the flash of forbidden thought out of his head. "I'm still stuffed. You?"

"Later, but I should probably look in on the kids now."

"Good plan."

"Sit down and relax. I'll put on some fresh coffee while I'm in there." Lana disappeared through the French doors leading through the dining room and beyond to the kitchen. Davis watched her until she disappeared from sight, unnervingly glad to see her again.

The ever-present work list—the one he and she had made together weeks ago—lay on a side table. Restless, he picked it up and ran a finger down the check marks. She had a long way to go on a complete remodel but the house was ready for winter. He was glad about that. He didn't like to think of her and Sydney in a draughty, cold house with frozen pipes.

The French door clicked open and Lana came to where he stood. His belly dipped again and he didn't deny his attraction. She smelled like flowers. Gardenias, he thought. In her heeled boots she reached his ear. Her reputation from long ago didn't matter to him at all, and he wondered if he should worry about that fact. Lana Ross had him by the heart.

"You've been busy," he said to her tilted face, gripping the notepad to keep his hands off her.

"Mostly I've painted and cleaned and ripped out old flooring."

"And put weather stripping around the doors and windows."

"Some of the doors and windows need replacing but there's no time for that now." She made a face. "Or money yet."

He laid aside the notepad and stuck his hands behind his back. "How's the *Gazette* job going?"

"Better. I think I'm getting the hang of this article-writing business. Saturday morning, I'm covering the Christmas Bazaar committee meeting. Saturday evening is the Cheerleaders' chili supper. Sunday, the Baptist Church is having its one hundredth birthday homecoming with a special speaker and a dedication of the new family center. I'm covering all those."

"I'm impressed."

"Me, too." She widened her eyes, laughing at herself. "So what have you been up to lately?"

"Thinking about you too much." The reply shocked her as much as it shocked him.

"Really?"

"I missed you."

"I'm right down the street."

The words flailed him, though her tone held no accusation. He was the one who'd withdrawn, not her. "If I had invited you to the Turner Thanksgiving feast, would you have come?"

"And given your sister a heart attack?" Lana smiled but her bottom lip trembled. Jenny's attitude hurt her, no matter how tough she tried to be.

Davis moved closer, finding her fingers. They felt cold. "Jenny's had some stuff going on, Lana. Not just with you. Her son is really sick."

Lana's chin came up, her eyes searching. "I didn't know that."

"He has a heart condition. I don't know the details. I just know he's been sickly all his life and is going to need another surgery real soon."

"I am so sorry." The cold fingers laced into his.

"Yeah. Me, too, but that's no excuse for her weird animosity against you."

"It's not exactly weird, Davis." She dropped her head. "I wasn't nice to her in high school."

He studied the top of her head, that pale strip of scalp where the dark brown hair parted. "Ancient history. Time to get over it."

"I guess."

"No guessing needed." He tilted her chin and gazed into her troubled eyes. "The rest of my family likes you. Especially me."

And then he didn't resist what he'd wanted to do for days. He kissed her.

Lana gripped the sides of Davis's jacket and gave herself to the kiss. His mouth was warm and tender like the man and tasted vaguely sweet like whipped topping. His chest, honed by work, was firm and strong, the perfect refuge for her personal storms. She wanted to sail into his safe harbor and stay. And oh, the way he kissed. The way his calloused hand cupped her cheek and threaded into her hair. She dropped her hands to his waist and around his back, snuggling closer.

She was dimly aware of the children's voices and a coffee smell drifting from the kitchen. But most of her senses were attuned to Davis, this man who didn't seem to have the good sense to stay away.

For two years, she'd steered clear of men, not trusting herself or them. Then along came Davis Turner to shatter her resolve.

A giggle broke through her fog. She jerked away from the warmth of Davis to find three children standing inside the French doors, eyes dancing, smiles a mile wide.

Oh, boy.

She shot a glance at Davis. Though his face was flushed, he allowed a sheepish grin and shrugged.

He cleared his throat and asked, "How was the pie?"

Paige and Sydney exchanged looks and giggled again. Then the three of them exchanged high fives and nearly fell over themselves as they ran out of the living room.

Lana started after them.

Davis caught her arm and pulled her back.

"But I need to explain...."

"Explain what, Lana? That we like each other? That I kissed you? I think they've figured that much out." He tugged her closer. "Now where were we?"

Lana was already shaking her head. This could not happen. She'd promised not to let it happen. Davis's sister was right about her whether Davis believed it or not. Lana knew too many things he didn't, especially about why his sister hated her.

"This is a bad idea, Davis." She stepped back, putting several feet between them though Davis didn't let go of her hand.

"I disagree. I wanted to kiss you a week ago."

"Why?"

He ran a frustrated hand through the top of his hair, sending it up into a wild spike. "Because I'm attracted to you. Is that so hard to imagine? Look at you. You're gorgeous and kind and we get along great. Come on. Give us a chance."

Lana's stomach churned. Her heart thundered louder than Digger Parsons's antique locomotive. She wanted to be with Davis more than he could ever know. Kissing him, being with him, was not like anything she'd experienced in her sordid past. With a man like Davis she almost felt clean. Almost.

With all her heart, she wished she could be the woman he needed, but he didn't know the real Lana Ross. The girl who'd drunk too much and slept around, who'd shoplifted and spent a few nights in jail, who'd basically kidnapped her niece and even now was hiding her out in Whisper Falls. Sure, he knew a little about her wild teen years, but his ardor would vanish like vapor if he learned everything.

She reached out and squeezed his fingers. "Let's go have a piece of your mother's pie. Okay?"

"No." He yanked his hand away and loomed over her. The hurt and confusion in his eyes clawed at her. "We're not ignoring this, Lana. I kissed you. You kissed me back. But it's not just about kissing." He grinned a small grin. "Though I have to admit kissing you was awesome. I want a relationship with you. We have something." When she stood there, unresponsive, he touched her face and said softly, "Cut me some slack here. Am I making a total fool of myself? Are you interested or not?"

His rough fingers were tender against her skin, melting her, muddling her conviction. "Yes, but—"

He put his hand over her mouth. "You said yes. That's good enough for now. No buts. Okay?"

Wanting to erase the hurt in his eyes, she nodded. How did she get out of this situation without hurting the most incredible man in her life?

She closed her eyes against the misgivings hammering at her conscience.

She needed time. Like a million years.

Chapter Eleven

The meeting of the Whisper Falls Christmas Bazaar Committee commenced Saturday morning in the conference room of the library, Miss Evelyn Parsons presiding. Lana arrived early, notebook and telephone recorder in hand to find others already there before her. She took a seat in back, heartened by the welcoming smiles of several familiar faces. Haley left her spot on the front row to sit next to Lana. She'd come alone.

"Where's your baby?" Lana asked.

"Daddy's play day." Haley smiled. "Creed loves having Rose to himself once in a while, and we already know his part in the bazaar. He works at my table and donates helicopter rides." She gave a little shiver. "Which I will never bid on."

Lana laughed at her friend's aversion. "You're so lucky."

"I know and I'm really thankful." Haley set a huge, lime-green tote bag on the floor. "How are things going with you and Mr. Looks-great-in-a-tool-belt?"

Lana rolled her eyes at the description though she had to agree. Davis in work clothes was every bit as attractive as Davis in church attire. She was still reeling from Thanksgiving Day and the feelings he'd stirred up inside her. For two days now she'd done nothing but wish for the impossible. "I think he likes me, Haley, and it won't work."

"Why?"

"You know why. We're all wrong for each other." When Haley only stared at her, head tilted, as if she was crazy, Lana admitted, "I stupidly let him kiss me."

"And?"

A slow grin pulled at Lana's cheeks. "It was amazing. *He's* amazing. And his kids are adorable but..."

"But you think you're not good enough because of all that junk from your past. That's it, isn't it?"

At that moment, several more people entered the room, among them Tara Brewster and Jenny Cranton. When Jenny saw Lana, she stiffened, grabbed Tara's elbow, leaned in and whispered something. Tara glanced at Lana, curiosity in her expression.

Shame rose in Lana.

"Who is that?" Haley asked.

"Davis's sister."

"Oh. Not good. Not good at all."

That was putting it mildly.

Others arrived, among them Annalisa and Cassie and a few other familiar faces in addition to some new ones. Head high, determined not to let Jenny's slight get to her, Lana introduced herself to the newcomers as a reporter for the *Gazette*.

Then the meeting commenced with Miss Evelyn in charge, efficiently setting up committees for everything from donations and advertising to volunteers and decorations. The bazaar, it seemed, was a very big event in Whisper Falls.

After a while, Miss Evelyn switched on some background Christmas music and the attendees split into groups to brainstorm and organize. Lana ventured from group to group, listening in, taking notes, gaining a buzz of excitement from the creativity flowing in the room. Had it not been for Jenny's coolness, Lana would have felt a part of the group. This was fun and fulfilling.

Kind of like kissing Davis Turner.

She shook her head at the random thought. The man gave her no rest at all. She knew she'd hurt his feelings on Thanksgiving, a truth that made her ache. She didn't want to hurt him. That was the whole point. But Davis, kind and wonderful Davis, had stayed another hour to eat pie and talk as if nothing had happened. When he'd left he'd kissed her on the cheek. That one little act—slow, sweet and powerful in its simple tenderness—had rocked her world.

Then, as if she hadn't felt like a big enough loser,

he'd called her yesterday. He'd found a Black Friday deal on bicycles for his kids and asked if she wanted one for Sydney's Christmas.

No wonder she couldn't stop thinking about him.

She shot a glance at Jenny's table. Davis's sister was busily writing something on a notepad but Tara Brewster glanced up, caught Lana's eye and smiled. Pleasantly surprised, Lana smiled back at the pretty blonde. The warm buzz increased and she moved on to the committee in charge of arts and crafts, Haley's group. As she listened in, she wished she had something to offer but creative arts were not her gift.

When they returned to full session, ideas fairly sizzled through the air to Miss Evelyn who fielded them all with alacrity. When no one volunteered for a task, Miss Evelyn appointed. And no one refused.

"Lana." The older woman peered over a pair of reading glasses. "I expect you to help with advertising."

Lana blinked a couple of times. "All right."

"Joshua Kendle isn't here but you ask him. He'll give us free space. Make us a pretty ad. Nice and big and run it often. Ted Beggs and I will take care of social media and the radio stations."

Now she understood how Miss Evelyn accomplished so much. With humor and strength, she delegated. Refusal was not an option. "Okay."

"Think about the music, too. The high school chorus is singing and the Methodist Choir. Maybe the Boggy Boys Band. But we could use you. Something modern and fresh and a little bit country."

Lana felt the stares turning in her direction. Haley gave her a thumbs-up. Thankfully, Miss Evelyn didn't push for a response, but simply said, "You think on it," and moved on to Edie, the owner of Sweets and Eats, who co-chaired the food and concessions.

Think on it? Her heart was pounding so hard, Lana couldn't think at all.

She bent to her notepad and pretended to write, missing several minutes of the meeting to calm her anxiety. Miss Evelyn surely must have heard about the incident at the basketball game and yet, she'd casually urged Lana to sing as if she hadn't made a fool of herself in front of several hundred people.

What was that about?

Ears buzzing, Lana scribbled madly, doodling little nothings.

Why couldn't she simply tell them the truth? Why couldn't she admit the reasons she wouldn't sing? But she knew the answer. They thought badly enough of her as it was. No way she'd admit that she couldn't sing sober.

After a bit, she shook off her dark thoughts to hear Miss Evelyn say, "This year we're reaching out, going for more tourist trade. Work your Facebook and Twitter." She tapped a pen against her lip. "Now if we could somehow promise them a white Christmas."

Titters of laughter trickled around the room. If anyone could wrangle snow from the sky for the sake of Whisper Falls tourism, Miss Evelyn would figure out a way.

A white-haired woman on the third row—Reverend Schmidt's wife—raised her hand. "Miss Evelyn? What is this year's charity?"

"Good question, Phoebe. Let me explain to the newcomers. Each year the town council chooses a charity to receive a portion of the money raised by the Christmas Bazaar. Townspeople may nominate an individual, a service group, or an outright charity such as missions. This year one of our own is in need."

Heads swiveled in the direction of Jenny's table. Curious, Lana watched as Jenny's face changed from puzzled to a slow dawning.

"Oh, my goodness," she said. "Oh, my. You didn't?"

Miss Evelyn's smile was benevolent. "We certainly did. You and Chuck put time and energy and love into this town. We want Charlie to have that operation ASAP."

"How did you know?" Jenny glanced left and right, expression incredulous, palms lifted. "We only found out ourselves yesterday."

"Don't you worry about that, hon, or anything else for that matter. God's taking care of that precious little boy of yours, and Whisper Falls will help with the rest."

Jenny covered her face with her hands and burst into tears. The women around her hugged her shoulders and patted her back. Tears glistened in more than one pair of eyes.

Lana was stunned. Davis had told her about Charlie's illness and the stress it had put on his sister, but she had never viewed Jenny as anything but a mean-spirited woman. Like Lana's mother. Whisper Falls apparently didn't see her that way.

The revelation shook her. Just as Jenny had judged her, she'd judged Jenny.

She still had a lot of growing to do.

As the meeting broke up, and Lana started to leave, mind reeling with this new information, Miss Evelyn called her name. "Lana, wait up, please."

Braced for more unwanted conversation about music, Lana nonetheless waited while other women huddled around Miss Evelyn like chicks around a hen. During the wait, she made a lunch date with Haley and chatted with Cassie and Annalisa and Pastor Ed. When a tear-streaked Jenny exited, surrounded by supportive friends, Lana felt the stirrings of compassion. In an odd kind of way, Lana understood the desire of a mother to do everything possible for the welfare of her child.

Soon the committee members cleared out, leaving only Lana, Haley and Miss Evelyn. Haley hitched her green tote and said, "Gotta run, ladies. See you at church tomorrow."

Church. Lana's heart thumped. Davis would be

there. After this revelation about Jenny, she was more flustered than ever. She lifted a hand and waved but Haley was already gone.

"I have a story idea for you," Miss Evelyn said without fanfare.

Some of the tension went out of Lana. No questions about the music. No pushy request for her to sing. Just a story idea. "Great. What is it?"

"The Christmas Express." Palm open, Miss Evelyn dramatically waved the word across the sky in a rainbow. "How's that sound?"

"Enticing. What is it?"

"Uncle Digger and I renamed the train for the holidays but we came up with this great idea kind of late, so we need you to write up a Jim-dandy article and spread the word."

Lana had stuffed the notebook in her tote but pulled it out again. "Tell me all about it."

"I have a better idea. We've gotten all the particulars in order for the inaugural ride which takes place tomorrow afternoon. Just a handful of invited people, mostly news folks. I even called the radio station down in Moreburg."

"You're inviting me along on the ride?"

"I sure am, though we could use more kiddies. You see, it's a family ride with lots of fun things for the children. You gather up that darling girl of yours and ask Davis to bring his children, too. Take lots of photos and write this up from the children's perspective."

Lana got stuck on the part about asking Davis. Would that be wise? Or would she be an even worse loser to let his children miss an opportunity to experience the brand-new Christmas Express?

"So what do you think? Isn't this a grand idea?" Lana looped her bag over her shoulder.

Oh, yeah. Just grand.

An Arctic front moved through the state late on Saturday night, chilling Sunday to freezing temperatures. Snow was in the forecast, much to the kids' delight. A sheen of lacy frost formed on windows and wood smoke puffed from atop houses, scenting the air as Davis stepped out of his truck. Car doors slammed and voices echoed over the parking spaces outside the train depot and museum. Below the town but visible from the depot, a handful of boats puttered along the shiny Blackberry River.

"Looks like a good turnout." Davis motioned with his chin toward the Channel Six news van.

"I saw some others pulling in, as well." Lana's lips puffed vapor. "Miss Evelyn mentioned a 'handful' of people but I think there might be a few more than that."

Davis shook his head, amused. Miss Evelyn had a way about her. "Any idea exactly what she has in mind?"

"Only what I told you on the phone. A *Polar Express* experience."

"You mean, like the movie?"

"We'll soon find out. Knowing Miss Evelyn and Uncle Digger, our evening will be way more than a train ride into the mountains." When they'd gotten out of the truck, Lana had taken Nathan's hand. Now she paused to tug his sock cap down over his ears, smiling. "Don't want your ears to freeze off."

Nathan giggled, eating up the attention.

The scene touched Davis in a way that had him wondering. Did Lana know the effect she had on his son? On him?

"It feels like Christmas," Paige said, hopping up and down in her thick, hooded parka. "This is going to be fun."

"A great way to start the Christmas season," Davis agreed.

The train depot sat in the center of town, a salute to the glory days of the railroad that had built Whisper Falls and other small Ozark towns round about. The 1920's passenger train, used for tourist excursions year-round, waited beyond the boardwalk steps. The engine's green-and-red paint had been transformed to Christmas colors by the addition of tiny lights and a giant wreath on the cowcatcher.

"Look," Sydney said, fairly bursting with excitement. Bundled in a bright blue coat that turned her eyes to gleaming jewels, Lana's little girl pointed to two red-clad characters standing in the train's open doorway. "Santa and Mrs. Claus!"

Sure enough Uncle Digger Parsons had traded

his usual striped overalls in favor of a red Santa suit and a snowy beard attached beneath his horseshoe mustache. On his head, though, was his engineer cap decorated with a sprig of holly. No doubt about it. Uncle Santa was driving this train. Miss Evelyn, cheeks rosy and eyes twinkling, wore a long red velvet dress, white apron and white hair covered by a ruffled red mobcap, a perfect Mrs. Claus.

Nathan stopped dead in his tracks. "Wow. Dad," he said in breathless awe. "This is so cool. An almost-real Santa."

The adults exchanged amused looks. Davis had always been truthful with his children about Santa Claus, not wanting them to confuse Santa and Jesus, but he'd never been militant about it.

"Sometimes pretending is fun," Lana said, kindly.

Nathan's earnest, innocent eyes raised to hers. "Can I pretend you're my mommy?"

Davis thought his heart would stop beating. Ever since some kid at school had asked him why his mother left, Nathan had craved the one thing Davis could not be. But his innocent blunder was both embarrassing and unanswerable. He'd put Lana in a tough spot and Davis didn't know how to help, especially after Thanksgiving. He still wondered why she'd invited them on today's outing. Surprised but glad.

Sorry, he mouthed over Nathan's head. Inside he

was praying she wouldn't break his son's heart, that she'd somehow let the little guy down easy.

In her snug jeans and brown fitted coat with glossy hair around her shoulders, Lana bent to cup Nathan's chin. "You are such a fine boy. Any woman would be honored."

Nathan looked from Lana to Davis, face twisted into a question mark. "Does that mean okay?"

His cute response broke the tension and both adults chuckled. A sudden lightness filled Davis's chest, and he felt relieved and grateful to the woman. Lana had done more than let Nathan down easy. She'd let him in.

He placed a hand on Nathan's shoulder and squeezed.

"Just like Santa Claus. We'll pretend for today." He wanted Nathan to have good memories of Christmas. The boy would learn soon enough that life—and love—were more complicated than a game of pretend.

With excited whoops, the children rushed ahead, climbing onto the train platform, not waiting for the adults. Miss Evelyn—aka Mrs. Santa—welcomed them. Uncle Digger disappeared inside but his ho-ho-ho echoed out into the late afternoon.

"Up you go." Davis put his hand beneath Lana's elbow as she took the first step, more because he wanted to touch her than because she needed help. "Thanks for the way you handled that," he said. "I'll have a talk with Nathan."

"He's just a little boy, Davis. He doesn't understand there is more to getting a mother than brown hair."

Davis gave a short huff. That was an understatement. Still, he was grateful to her. "Missed you at church this morning."

"It's nice to be missed." She didn't offer an explanation and before he could ask, she gasped. "Look at this place."

He did. The interior of the old train had been turned into a Christmas spectacular. Bright red stars and huge snowflakes dangled from a rounded ceiling festooned with lighted garland. The side posts looked like red-and-white peppermint sticks. Swags of shiny tinsel dipped from one side of the car to the other. More silver tinsel had been roped along the backs of the seats and topped with bright red bows. Christmas music seeped through the speakers, quiet but cheery. It was an over-the-top wonderland of Christmas, missing only the snow and presents.

"I've ridden the train before during the fall foliage tours, but this is something."

Lana lifted her nose and looked around. "Do you smell cinnamon?"

He took a long sniff, filling his lungs with a smell that reminded him of Mom's Christmas cookies. "I think it's coming through the vents. Nice touch."

"It's making me hungry for a cinnamon roll!"

Lana said with a laugh, her eyes sparkling. She looked fresh and pretty and full of joy today. He liked the look. In fact, he liked a lot of things about Lana Ross and unless his male radar had gone completely bust, she liked him, too. They got along great, could talk about anything and they liked each other's kids. So why did she push him away every time he ventured near?

The cars were filling rapidly and the same gush of excited pleasure escaped from many of the riders as they found their seats. Miss Evelyn and Uncle Digger had outdone themselves and the trip hadn't even begun.

Davis and Lana followed the children, coming to rest in the center of the car with the kids in a front seat and the two adults behind. Davis was certain the three munchkins had intentionally maneuvered him and Lana into sharing a seat. He had to admit sitting next to Lana in a seat built for the smaller bodies of 1920's riders was pretty cozy. Their shoulders brushed and Lana's flowery fragrance messed with his head. And when she turned her head the tiniest bit, they were as close as a whisper.

While he was enjoying the attraction, Uncle Digger's voice came over the intercom calling, "All aboard for the Christmas Express!" The train lurched once before slowly chugging out of the depot. "Settle back and enjoy the ride, folks. We're on our way to the North Pole!"

"North Pole!" A wide-eyed Paige squealed and grabbed Sydney in a mutual little-girl hug. "North Pole!"

Nathan, crammed against the window, whipped around. "Dad, guess what? We're going to the North Pole. Right now!"

Davis's mouth lifted. "So I heard. I'm sure glad we brought our coats."

"Yeah." His boy looked from Davis to Lana. "You can snuggle up if you get too cold."

Davis laughed. "I'll keep that in mind." Snuggling with Lana sounded pretty good, if he thought about it. Which he did. "Look out the window, buddy."

Easily distracted, the excited boy whipped around and pressed his face into the window. Rings of vapor clouded the pane. He swiped at them with his coat sleeve and watched the town slip away.

Miss Evelyn and her helpers, all appropriately dressed in elf attire, moved through the cars handing out candy canes and programs.

Lana took out her camera and said, "I should get some photos. Will you excuse me?"

"What? No snuggling?" he teased.

She stuck a finger in his face. "You have to wait until we reach the North Pole. Remember?"

Her lighthearted reply tickled him. He stood to let her out of the seat, grinning when she leaned around to face the kids, camera at the ready. "All right, you three, say cheese."

The children hammed it up, giggling, crossing their eyes and poking out pink tongues. Laughing, too, Lana snapped and snapped before moving on to other children in their car, taking the time to gather names and permission. He watched her, interested in the genuinely nice way she had about her. Lana had changed a lot in her years away. The name was the same but the woman wasn't.

The classic song, "Rockin' Around the Christmas Tree" came through the speakers. Lana began to bebop toward him, mouthing the words.

He thought about her music and knew she missed it. On Thanksgiving she'd played the guitar and sang with the children in her rich mezzo-soprano voice. Her gift was meant to be shared whether she was a big star or not. Though she claimed stage fright, he couldn't stop thinking there was more, something she hadn't told him.

Lana had secrets.

Suddenly, she stuck the camera in his face and before he could recover from the shock, she pressed the shutter button.

"Hey!"

"My boss likes lots of photos and so do the readers."

"The only person who will like that one is my mother."

"There you go then. One happy reader." Full of energy and Christmas cheer, she scooched him with her shoulder and hip, pushing him to the in-side of the seat. The mountains outside the win-dow were brown and bare except for the glades of deep green pines and cedar. Occasionally a vivid red cardinal flitted through the trees.

"I want to sit with you, Daddy," Nathan said after a while. Davis wasn't surprised. His boy had never been good at long-distance rides.

Lana patted the tiny space between them. "Come on back. We'll make room."

Crawling over the girls, he came, crowding into the narrow spot.

"Tired of riding, little man?" Lana asked.

"Yeah." Candy cane in his mouth, he leaned against her, slowly inching down as if to put his head in her lap. Davis considered stopping him but Lana didn't seem to mind.

She gathered Nathan close as if holding Davis's growing eight-year-old was the natural thing for her to do. When Nathan grew too warm, she helped him with his coat, murmuring something in his ear that made him smile around the peppermint stick.

Davis's insides clenched. His children adored Lana and she treated them with such tender con-sideration it took his breath. She was good for them. There was nothing sweeter to a dad than knowing a woman cared about his children.

They'd ridden a while when Miss Evelyn an-nounced a sing-along and familiar Christmas songs filtered through the speakers. Nathan sat up then,

candy cane still in his mouth to sing "Jingle Bells."
The elves came through the car handing out bell
bracelets for the children to shake. And shake them,
they did!

Paige whipped around in her seat and, above the
noise said, "Sing, Dad. Sing, Lana."

Davis obliged, pleased when Lana's husky voice
joined in. The sound really was rough honey, flowing over him sweet and thick with a touch of gravel
that raised goose bumps on his arms.

When the song ended, he leaned toward her.
"Your voice knocks me out. You still love to sing,
don't you?"

"I do. I shouldn't. I promised God I'd lay it down
if He'd—" She stopped again and shook her head.
"Never mind."

"If He would do what?"

A beat passed and he could see the wheels turning in her head. Would she lie to him or share a
little glimpse of herself?

"If He would change my life. And He did."

"Do you really think God doesn't want you to
use your talent?"

"It was the only thing I had to trade." She dropped
her gaze to Nathan's shirt collar. Davis caught her
hand, pulled her around to face him. "You think
the stage fright came from God?"

"No. Maybe." She heaved a heavy sigh and
moved her hand back to Nathan. "I don't know
where it came from, Davis, but my life is better

now. Sharing my music with strangers is behind me. I'm happy."

If that was true Davis had made a mistake that could come back to bite him.

"Deck the Halls" broke out over the gathering, led by a slightly off-key but no less enthusiastic Miss Evelyn. Davis dropped a friendly arm around Lana's shoulders and hugged. "Then make me happy, too. Sing. Sing like nobody's listening."

So she did. As the music fell from their lips, Paige looked over one shoulder to listen. Seeing Davis with his arm around Lana, she punched Sydney. Both girls turned to grin. Above the music, Sydney pumped her fist and proclaimed, "Now that's what I'm talking about!"

Chapter Twelve

The North Pole proved to be every bit as exciting as the train ride.

Though enjoying the pleasure of Davis's company too much, Lana let herself go with the moment for the sake of the children. They were having such a grand time. Hadn't she told Nathan that today they could pretend all they wanted? She could pretend she wasn't the town party girl and that she deserved the attention of a good man like Davis. She could even pretend that Sydney was her daughter and neither would ever again have to worry about the authorities taking her away.

By the time the train stopped in what she knew was another small town over the mountains, the sun had set. They disembarked beneath a giant sign proclaiming The North Pole, where a wonderland of light displays circled a small man-made lake. Halfway around the walking track, on the opposite side of the glistening water, a warming hut painted in bright colors was labeled Santa's Workshop.

"Oh, this is perfect," she murmured and started toward the winding trail. "Look, kids, you can write letters to Santa."

"Wait!" Nathan's urgent voice stopped her in midstride. He grabbed Lana, tugging her back to Davis's side. Then, he pulled them closer until they'd clasped gloved hands.

"There. That's better." The little guy was persistent. She'd give him that.

She glanced at Davis who shrugged, his eyes twinkling as with merriment. "Can't argue with pretend."

Right. Pretend. She could do that. She let herself enjoy the strength of Davis's gloved hand.

Nathan insisted on holding Lana's other hand and Davis reached out to Sydney, an act that made the child light up brighter than the light displays. On the far end, Paige grabbed onto her new best friend, and all five of them were connected by a bridge of fingers.

"This is nice," she said, meaning it.

They looked like a family, strolling through the displays, exclaiming over the animations. A happy family.

Waving elves and a blinking Rudolph gave way to whimsical displays by businesses. Nathan giggled at an animated toothbrush sponsored by a dentist and at the Elvis-Santa driving a car from the local dealership.

With their cheeks and noses rosy cold, they stopped at a nativity set up by a local church. There they were serenaded by a group of carolers, bundled against the cold to sing along to a portable stereo. Lana snapped more photos, committing the scene to memory. How would she ever put all this into one article? When she replaced the camera in her tote, Davis took her hand again. She let him.

The evening was beautiful, cold and clear, the kind she'd dreamed of where a mother and father took their children out to make Christmas memories.

A silly dream but as sweet as the peppermint on her tongue.

When their toes began to tingle, they stopped inside Santa's Workshop to warm up. Here the children scribbled letters to Santa before sliding them into a big red mailbox marked *S. Claus.*

All too soon, the train whistle announced the time of departure. The children groaned. Lana felt like doing the same. Like Cinderella at the ball, her time with Prince Charming was drawing to a close.

"Too much fun," Davis said, smiling at the dejected trio of children.

"Can we come back again?" Even Paige's snazzy freckles lost their cheer.

Davis's gaze found Lana's. "Maybe," he said,

sending a wild root of hope shooting through her heart.

She was being ridiculous and she knew it. When she got home, she'd remind herself of all the reasons she was not good for Davis and his kids. But not now, not when the evening had become nothing short of a fairy tale.

With light hearts and more protests from the children, they moved with the crowd back onto the train. The kids were tired. The excitement had taken a toll. They crowded into their seat, quieter but still talking about the wonders of the light displays.

After the train rolled on again, chugging smoothly through the deep forest and over Blackberry Mountain toward Whisper Falls, a pair of elves passed out foam cups of hot chocolate loaded with mini-marshmallows. The overhead lights dimmed, bathing everyone in shadows. Toward the front of the car, Miss Evelyn sat under a spotlight on a high stool and read a Christmas story. Lana suspected the elves read similar stories in the remaining cars.

The rocking of the train and Miss Evelyn's story lulled the passengers, including herself. More than one woman leaned her head on the shoulder of the man beside her. Lana was tempted to do the same.

The semilit car created an air of privacy as though dozens of other people weren't sitting nearby. She felt cocooned between the cool window and the warm, masculine man.

Mellowed by the thoughts, she sipped at her cocoa, the taste sweet on her tongue.

"Mustache," Davis murmured, leaning close enough to make her pulse misbehave.

"Hmm?" she asked, head tilted toward him.

In the shadows he leaned closer, grinning. He touched her upper lip. "Marshmallow mustache."

"Oh." Before she could raise her hand to clear it away, Davis touched his lips to hers. Tender, sweet and over too quickly.

"I think I got it for you." His grin had become a gentle, quizzical smile. His eyes held questions though Lana had no adequate answers.

"Great." She touched her mouth, breathless. One very innocent, friendly kiss and she could hardly think straight.

"Let me know if I didn't." He winked. "Or better yet, have another drink."

Have another drink. The old familiar phrase meant something different in Lana's world than marshmallow-laden cocoa.

She'd had too many drinks too many times with too many different men. Though she'd not touched alcohol for nearly two years, she couldn't forget what it had done to her.

She squeezed Davis's arm in an apology he would never understand and turned to stare out at the passing night.

* * *

"Hey."

Not this time. This time she talked to him. If she was going to shut him down, she was going to give him a reason.

Davis took Lana by the shoulder and gently tugged.

She turned her head, her hair swishing against her sweater, her eyebrows lifted in question. "Hmm?"

"What's going on? You invited me on this trip. We've had a terrific time. At least I have. I thought you were enjoying yourself, too."

"I am."

"Then what's the deal? Why do you disappear like that?"

Her head tilted. "Did I?"

He gave an annoyed sigh. "Are you intentionally trying to frustrate me?"

"Why would I do that?"

"I don't know. That's why I'm asking. I like you, Lana. You know I do. I'm a guy. You're a girl. It's only natural that I'd want to kiss you."

She closed her eyes as if his words were too hard to hear. Her rusty voice sounded small and tired. "I like you, too."

"Good." He pulled her unresisting hand into his. "Let's start over then. I like you. You like me. Life is good."

"It's not that simple."

"Then explain it to me because I must be slow.

Maybe I'm too dumb or out of practice to get the message when a woman is giving me the brush-off." He sounded testy, even to himself. So, okay, he *was* testy. She was making him crazy.

"I'm not trying to... Today has been—" she searched for the words, staring around the darkened train "—a beautiful dream."

His anger dissolved, fizzled, died. "For me, too. You, me, these kids. Pretty special stuff."

"Yes." The affirmation was a mere breath but he heard it.

He heard something else. too, a yearning that was answered deep in his heart. At that moment, he thought he understood. "You're scared."

She offered a small smile. "Terrified."

His protective gene activated. "Don't be. It's just me, your friendly neighborhood handyman, and you, the most amazing woman I've met in a long time. We can handle anything together."

And I think I'm in love with you.

He didn't say that, of course, but the words coursed through his veins, like a steady beat of his heart.

"Oh, Davis." Lana turned completely away from the window to lay her head on his shoulder.

Now they were getting somewhere. He didn't know what dragons she battled, but he wanted to slay them all.

He found her cheek and caressed the soft, smooth skin. "Give us a chance. Okay?"

She sighed, a warm, breathy, marshmallow sigh against his jaw. After a painfully long moment, she nodded. "I'd like that."

Her admission slammed into him with g-force. Finally.

Davis figured he might as well test the waters. See if she meant it. He touched her cheek, her eyelids, her mouth. And then he kissed her again.

Mr. Kendle loved the Christmas Express article. So much so that he gave Lana a byline and a small raise in pay.

Feeling happier than she could remember, Lana walked with a purposeful stride down Easy Street, the chilly breeze in her hair and the smell of the river in her nose. Her boot heels tapped music on the sidewalk. Her red scarf lifted on the breeze, bouncing against her faux-leather coat, as if to keep the beat.

Yesterday had been wonderful. The ending had been even better. For a few minutes guilt had tried to ruin the day, but Davis had pushed his way past her shame and given her hope.

Maybe she could be different. Maybe she could let go of the past. Maybe she could love and be loved by a good man.

Did she dare believe?

Her years in music had made her a night owl and last night, long after Sydney was asleep, she'd stayed up so buoyed by hope and happiness that she'd written another new song from start to finish. A love song.

This morning the music poured through her mind and soul. She hummed as she did errands and gathered ideas for future articles, enjoying the blast of holiday music coming from a bullhorn speaker above Classy Girls Boutique.

A short time later she drove to Haley Carter's home for the promised lunch date. The Carters lived on the edge of town on a small acreage surrounded by trees and an enormous garden. Various garden plots lay all around the house, though they were mostly sleeping under mulch for the winter months.

Everything about the white frame cottage screamed, "artsy." Haley's folk art was visible on the porch, in the yard and gardens and inside the house.

"Come on in," Haley called before Lana could knock. "I have my hands in dough."

Having visited before, Lana knew the way and passed through the living room to the kitchen. Baby Rose sat on the floor banging a spoon against a plastic bowl. Haley stood at the counter mixing a fragrant dough. Flour powdered the front of her green blouse.

"Bread?" Lana asked. "Smells great."

Haley scratched her chin against her shoulder, hands deep in the dough. "The fabulous tree ornaments we're making for the bazaar."

"You really think you can teach me well enough that people will buy them?"

Haley hitched her chin toward Lana's coat. "Take off your coat, roll up your sleeves and we'll find out. Lesson one in progress while lunch bakes."

Lana did as she was told and soon had her hands in the soft, elastic dough.

"I hear you had a date with Davis last night."

"How did you hear—" Lana shook her head. "Never mind. This is Whisper Falls." She told Haley a little about the Christmas Express. "You and Creed should go."

"It sounds fun. We will. But that's not the part I wanted to know. Tell me about you and Davis. Did you have fun together?"

"We did." Lana smiled down in the dough. "We really did."

Haley had her back turned but she spun around, eyes wide with sudden comprehension. "I think you're falling in love with him."

Lana tweaked a shoulder. "Maybe."

"Oh, you are. I know the symptoms. Just look at the way you sparkle and the energy pouring out of you. I bet you wrote another song."

Lana's mouth dropped open. "How did you know that?"

"Because falling in love made me more creative. It's what artists do. If we're sad, we create. If we're happy, we create. But love is the best motivator of all."

"Davis invited Sydney and me to go with them to the Blackwell's Ranch. He and his kids cut their own Christmas tree from the woods. Apparently, it's a tradition he started after his wife died. And he asked us to go along."

"You're going, of course."

"Well, yeah. Sydney and I need a Christmas tree, too."

They both laughed and Haley bumped Lana's side with hers.

Lana needed more than a Christmas tree. She needed to have her head examined. Sooner or later, she and Davis must have a long, open conversation about some very painful subjects. If their budding relationship was to have a chance, he'd have to know everything, even the worst. He deserved to know.

But today she was too happy, too hopeful to worry about the ugly darkness in her past.

"We're going on horseback?"

The surprise on Lana's face was exactly what Davis had expected.

The five of them had arrived at the Blackwell Ranch on a cold Saturday, eager to cut fresh Christmas trees, and now, they were walking toward a large, dirt corral. A light dusting of snow covered the ground like powdered sugar on cake.

Davis allowed a small, teasing grin. "Did I forget to mention the horses?"

Lana squinted her eyes at him in pretend anger. "Yes, you did."

"Is that a problem? You're not scared of horses or anything, are you?"

"No. Well, maybe a little. They are awfully big. But it sounds…adventurous. I *am* dressed for it." She glanced down at her jeans and cowboy boots, the latter older and lower-heeled than he'd seen her wear before. "But Sydney's wearing tennies."

"So is Paige. We aren't going far and Austin's horses are used to kids. They don't care what's on your feet."

"And how would you know that?" she asked. "Do the horses speak to you? Do they tell you all their secrets?"

He liked when she joked around. Today she was light and easy and sparkling. "Nothing as mysterious as that. Nathan went through a horse obsession last year. Austin gave him lessons for a while on old Tinker. All three of us got to do some riding."

"All my animals are gentle as overgrown dogs." Austin came out of the barn, leading a pair of horses, a large bay and a buckskin. Austin was a tall man, taller than Davis by several inches though the boots added a couple more. Broad and well-muscled in a rough-hewn leather coat and white cowboy hat, Austin was a quiet man with a big presence. Davis was proud to call him friend. "Ever ridden before?"

"I actually have." Lana eased toward the bay,

gloved hand extended. "A friend of mine owned a ranch outside Nashville. But I haven't in a long time."

It was one of the few times she'd mentioned her life in Tennessee. Davis was curious to know more, to know everything about the woman who was rapidly invading his heart and life.

The ride on the Christmas Express had done him in. Since that night, he thought about her all the time, smelled her gardenia perfume in his sleep and spent every free moment at her house. Most of the time the two of them worked on the house while the three kids romped like cubs or did homework. Sometimes they just hung out. They watched TV together, played checkers—always a formidable match—or listened to music. Often Lana would sing for him—spurts and starts of whatever composition she was working on, slightly self-conscious because the song wasn't finished, but wistful and dreamy. He wondered if she'd eventually return to Nashville. If she even wanted that. He didn't know much about music, but he knew what he liked to hear. If Lana wanted another shot at the stars, he wanted it for her.

Davis caught her elbow. "Are you sure you're okay with the horses? If you're not, we can walk. It's no big deal."

Her smile convinced him. But then that smile of hers could turn his brain to vanilla pudding. "The kids will love going by horseback, Davis. A memory to treasure forever."

"That's what I thought." The five of them looked like a family making memories together.

"Come over here, Sydney." Lana reached back to where the kids hopped and danced and ran in circles like animations. Smoky vapor exited their noses, three fire-breathing dragons. Sydney stopped immediately to obey. "Put your hand out. Let the horse smell you."

"Like dogs do?"

"Exactly."

The little girl, her curly brown hair poking from beneath a hooded coat, eagerly offered her palm. Both horses leaned in, naturally curious, for a sniff. Sydney giggled, a sound that touched Davis for some reason. She was a shy, sweet little girl with a great giggle. He wondered if she'd ever wanted a dad the way Nathan wanted a mom.

Not to be left out, Nathan and Paige let the horses sniff, and then rubbed their gloved hands down the noble necks.

"If you'll hold on to these," Austin said, "I'll see if Annalisa has the other two saddled."

"Is she going with us?"

"She wouldn't miss it, but Cassie will. She's working." Cassie was his single sister. She lived on the ranch, too. "Saturday is a big day at the shop."

"I thought Annalisa was expecting a baby?" Lana said.

This was news to Davis, but Austin's chest expanded at the mention. A grin spread across Davis's face. He remembered that feeling, the pride and joy.

"Doc says the exercise is good for her. For both of them." Still grinning like a new daddy, Austin pivoted toward the barn.

Davis followed, willing to help with the animals.

"We still on to get that bathroom retiled?" the cowboy asked.

"Next week maybe." Davis narrowed his eyes to think through his schedule. He knew Austin wanted the work done before Christmas, as a gift to his wife. "Is that soon enough?"

"Yup."

The large barn smelled of hay and leather and horse flesh. Annalisa, a saddle blanket in her hands, smiled at her husband. The big rancher visibly melted, a teddy bear where his wife was concerned. It was a beautiful thing, Davis thought, the love between a man and a woman. A very beautiful thing.

Soon the horses were saddled, and the party mounted. Austin's big bay, a horse he called Cisco, was loaded with gear. He and Annalisa led the way. Davis and Lana brought up the rear. With the children sandwiched between the adults, they headed up a well-traveled trail into the mountainous forest spreading around and beyond the Blackwell Ranch.

Lana rode at Davis's flank. He thought she handled a horse pretty well, if a little stiffly. Sydney bounced up and down on Tinker, the old gelding with the gentle spirit.

To reassure both Lana and the little girl, Davis said, "He'll take care of her. Don't worry."

The horses trudged with practiced ease, heads down and bobbing up the incline through hickory and oak. As the trail steepened, conical evergreens began to dot the landscape. They'd journeyed only a short distance, less than a mile, when Austin raised a leather-clad hand to stop.

Lana sucked in a breath as a doe and fawn bolted from the brush, crossed the trail in front of them and then leaped into the trees on the opposite side. Not one of the horses reacted other than an ear flicker.

"Beautiful," Lana breathed.

Davis stared at the side of her face. "Sure is."

"Dad, Dad, did you see that?" In wide-eyed wonder, Paige drew his attention. "A mama and a baby deer."

He understood the thrill. Even as an adult, he found the grace and beauty of white-tailed deer a sight to behold. His kids would talk about it for days.

Austin dropped his hand and the journey continued, ending in a thick stand of evergreen.

"Here we are," Austin announced as he dismounted and walked back to lift his wife tenderly from the horse. When Annalisa's feet touched the ground, the big cowboy lowered his head and kissed her.

Davis couldn't help looking at Lana. What would she think if he did the same? But before he could act on the impulse, she was off the buckskin, helping the children dismount.

Once the horses were secured, Annalisa swept her arms in a wide arc around the glade. "Pick your Christmas tree. There are plenty."

"Too many," Austin said with a frown. "Can't graze cattle on juniper."

Annalisa laughed, her blond beauty enhanced by her early pregnancy. Not that Davis could even tell she was expecting other than the happy glow.

Nathan, Paige and Sydney made a beeline through the trees, exclaiming over first one evergreen and then another. The adults trudged along, grinning at the childish excitement.

"I want a giant one. Tall as the ceiling," Nathan exclaimed, stretching his arms as high as possible. "Big as the sky."

"How about you, Lana?" Davis asked. "Want one big as the sky?"

"Bigger." Her blue eyes sparkled in the winter sunlight. She slipped her hand into the crook of his elbow.

Blood humming with pleasure, Davis put a hand over her fingers and squeezed gently. His heart was doing funny things, happy things, inside his chest. "Whatever the lady wants."

She turned her head to look at him and he leaned in to kiss the corner of her mouth. Her smile widened and she returned the favor, her lips warm against his cold cheek.

This was good. Really good.

He could imagine himself with Lana, searching for the perfect tree, year after year. Could she imagine it, too?

"How about this one?" Nathan shouted, drawing their focus, though Davis's heart continued to dance to music no one could hear but him.

Up ahead, Paige and Sydney were slowly circling a tall, stately cedar while Nathan, nose red, ran back to Austin for the ax.

"This is it. This is it!" he called.

"Remember, we need two."

"Make that three," Annalisa said. "I think you've picked a good one, though." She circled the tree with the children, hands on hips. "No gaps. Nice and cone shaped. Very green."

"It's beautiful." Sydney had removed a glove and was testing the branches as she talked to Paige. "And it smells really good. I think it's kind of perfect. You and Nathan can have this one."

Her generosity touched a tender spot in Davis. Truth was Sydney got to him as much as her mother did. He'd seen her let Nathan have the first turn or the last cookie. Generous, caring. Like Lana.

Why had he ever wondered about Lana's mothering skills? She'd done an amazing job with Sydney.

"It *is* kind of perfect," he said, taking the ax from Nathan as Austin and Annalisa moved deeper into the woods in search of their own perfect Christmas tree. "Who gets the first whack?"

"You chop it, Daddy." Paige grabbed Sydney's coat sleeve and dragged her backward from the tree.

"I want to help." Nathan stuck close to his dad. "I'll hold the tree so it won't fall down. Huh, Dad?"

Before Davis could give the warning, Nathan stuck his bare hand into the prickly limbs of the cedar. He let out a yowling cry and jerked back.

Davis dropped the ax and reached for his son. To his surprise, Nathan threw himself into Lana's waiting arms, tears falling.

"Shh. Let me see. Let me see, sugar." Lana knelt on the cold ground to look at Nathan's hand. "There now. It's only a sticker."

Nathan stopped crying and blinked dark, wet lashes. His lip quivered but he was trying to be brave. "Can you get it out? It hurts me."

"I think I can," Lana said, "Will you hold real still while I try? I promise to be careful."

Trusting, Nathan nodded. He sniffed one long sniff and said, "Okay."

By now, Davis was on his knees next to the pair and Sydney and Paige hovered as though Nathan had lost a limb.

Using her fingernails, Lana carefully extracted a half-inch splinter from Nathan's palm. Then, while

Davis watched with his heart in his throat, she placed a kiss on the dirty spot.

"How's that feel? Better?"

Nathan, his face inches from hers, nodded. With a long sniffing shudder, he said, "I love you, Lana."

Lana's eyelids dropped shut. She pulled his baby into her arms and murmured, "I love you, too, sugar."

Davis put his arms around the pair of them, heart bursting, the scent of cedar in his nose and wild hope in his chest.

Chapter Thirteen

Who knew decorating a Christmas tree could be both romantic and hilarious?

Lana smiled up at Davis as she dug through a plastic shopping bag of brand-new decorations. There had been a box of old ones in the attic but she was starting fresh. No need to drag out bad memories. Especially of the Christmas Mama had slapped Tess for sneaking a present and her parents had fought far into the night. That was the year Daddy went to work one day and never came home again.

She shook her head, abolishing dark thoughts from the perfect evening. The fireplace crackled. They'd made popcorn and put on a Christmas CD of kids' songs. Most importantly, people she cared about were present.

"Thank you for this," she said. "Decorating this tree means a lot to Sydney."

They'd left Davis's tree propped against the side

of the side of his garage in a bucket of water, agreeing to decorate Sydney's lopsided wonder first.

"What about her mom?"

Her conscience tweaked. She should tell him Sydney was not her child, but now didn't seem the right time. Soon, though, she promised. Soon.

She simply said, "It means a lot to her, too." Wherever she is. "Decorating yours tomorrow gives us another good excuse to get together and have fun."

Davis, a strand of glittery tinsel in his calloused hands, moved closer. He jacked a sandy eyebrow. "Do we need an excuse?"

Lana's pulse jumped. She studied his eyes, saw the affection in their depths and marveled. "No," she answered. "I don't think we do."

At moments like this, Lana wanted to pinch herself. Davis Turner, the nicest guy on the planet, wanted to be with her. Plenty of men had been attracted to her, but not like this. When Davis touched or kissed her, she felt clean, unused. She felt new again.

He draped a length of tinsel around her neck and slowly drew her to him. When she laughed, he rubbed her nose with his and laughed, too.

From her peripheral vision, she saw the children approach and tried to pull away. But Davis held her fast.

"Too late," he said. "You can't escape the inevitable."

She glanced around, not understanding. The

three matchmakers grinned from ear to ear as Paige stretched tall to hold a branch of plastic mistletoe over their heads.

"You're right," she answered, moving back into his space. "Far too late."

Davis was standing at his kitchen sink scrubbing paint from beneath his fingernails when his front door burst open. Expecting Jenny with his kids, he didn't bother to turn around until Paige rushed to his side and burst into great heaving sobs.

"Oh, Daddy!"

Davis jerked his hands from beneath the flow of warm water, splashing the cabinets and floor. "Hey! What's going on here?"

Paige was not one to wail and cry, but before she could pull herself together, an agitated Jenny plowed through the doorway with Nathan and Kent in tow, their eyes wide and worried. Charlie was nowhere to be seen.

The noise in the room was worse than a jack-hammer on concrete. Paige crying. Jenny talking. Davis asking what was going on. Nathan grabbed onto his daddy's leg and clung like a spider monkey.

Fear snaked up Davis's spine.

"What's wrong? Where's Charlie? Has something happened?"

The noise grew louder as everyone started talking at once. Finally, he stuck his fingers in his mouth and whistled like a referee. The noise ceased.

"Will someone tell me what's going on before I call 9-1-1?"

"That woman is a kidnapper."

This statement from Jenny started the sobs in Paige again.

"I didn't mean to tell, Daddy. Sydney made me promise. It was an accident."

"Who's a kidnapper? You didn't mean to tell what?" The hysteria was starting to scare him.

Jenny put a hand on Paige's shoulder. "Honey, you did the right thing. Now, go wash your face and calm down while I speak to your daddy. None of this is your fault."

Paige looked from Jenny to Davis. When Davis nodded reassuringly, she trudged out of the kitchen, shoulders drooping.

"You boys go in the living room and watch TV while Aunt Jenny and I talk," Davis said. Hands still dripping on the floor, he grabbed a dish towel. Whatever was going on, he didn't need crying, clinging children involved.

Once the boys were dispatched, he wiped his hands and said, "All right. What's going on? Is Charlie all right?"

"He's in the car. No worse than usual. That's not why I'm here."

"Is anyone hurt?"

"Not physically." When he hitched a hip in a get-on-with-it stance, his sister said, "Paige told me something about Sydney and Lana today that

I think you should know before you get any more involved with them."

He straightened, suddenly wary. Any more involved and they'd be standing before a preacher.

A bad feeling snaked up the back of his neck. "I won't listen to gossip about her, Jenny. She's changed."

"I'm not repeating gossip. Paige let something slip today that Sydney wasn't supposed to tell. It's crucial you know or I wouldn't be here." She looked toward the ceiling and back as if searching for the right words. "I'm your sister. I want what's best for you. I know things about Lana Ross that I won't bring up because as you said, they happened in high school. But this is happening now, and it's too important to brush aside just because you have the hots for her."

He clenched his fists, mouth going from dry to tight. "I think I resent your implication."

"If I'm speaking out of turn, I'm sorry. Nathan told me about all the kissing and snuggling that's been going on lately."

"Which does not translate to anything inappropriate, if that's what you're implying. You've nagged me for a year about dating. I like Lana. A lot." He sucked in a breath. "I might even be in love with her."

That silenced her for all of five seconds.

"Oh, Davis. It breaks my heart to see you hurt

again. Lana has misled you. She's lied to you. She's used you to get her house remodeled."

"Gee, thanks, sis." He laid on the sarcasm. "A man likes to know what his sister thinks about his ability to attract women."

"I didn't mean that. You could have had a nice woman in Tara, but you're like a moth to the flame."

"I'm not a moth. I'm a man. Now, either spit it out or go home. Paige needs me."

Jenny brushed a tired hand over her forehead. "Lana Ross may be a criminal."

His brow lowered in disbelief. Lana, a criminal? Not a chance. "What did she do, forget to return a library book? Double-park on Easy Street?"

As if she truly did not want to tell him, Jenny swallowed and looked away, shaking her head in regret. "Oh, Davis. Oh, my brother. Sydney is not Lana's child. She brought her here under false pretenses."

The revelation was like being hit in the face with a bucket of ice water. He went cold all over.

"What are you talking about? Of course, Sydney's her child. Why would Lana lie about a thing like that?" Particularly since he'd asked about Sydney's father and she'd told him an uncomfortable truth.

"I don't know, Davis. Perhaps you should ask Lana outright. Or better yet, call the authorities in Nashville."

His head buzzed with the information. It couldn't be true. Could it? "Paige told you this?"

"Don't blame the child. She didn't mean to let the cat out of the bag. She was devastated, as you could see, to have betrayed a confidence." Jenny reached in the pocket of her slacks and withdrew a tissue. "Apparently, child welfare was threatening to put Sydney into foster care because of her mother's lifestyle so Lana ran away with her. Drugs, I gather."

"Lana? Drugs?" He dropped his chin and wagged his head back and forth. "Not even close to being true." He was sure, wasn't he?

"No, Lana wasn't the one doing drugs. It was Sydney's *real* mother."

"Sydney's real mother?" He grabbed the back of his head with one hand, his nerves fraying. "Who *is* Sydney's real mother? And what does Lana have to do with any of it?"

"She brought Sydney here to escape the authorities. That's all I know. Paige was fuzzy on the particulars. I suggest you speak to Lana, although if she lied once, she'll lie again." Tears glistened in her eyes. "I'm sorry, Davis. You and the kids have been through so much. I didn't want you to be hurt by that woman. Please don't be angry at me for telling you. You have a right to know."

Yes, he did. He had a right to honesty.

Jenny was his sister, a good woman with a lot on her plate. He trusted her. She wouldn't tell him something unless she believed it was true. She might not like Lana but she cared about him and his kids.

He tossed the dishtowel on the counter. His whole body trembled. His heart raced like a juiced thoroughbred's. He didn't know what was going on up the street, but he intended to find out. Now.

Lana strummed her guitar, softly singing the newly composed tune. Funny how the house she'd hated had become a house of hope. When her work was done for the day, she loved sitting on the wide hearth with the fire at her back as she wrote articles or music or prayed, full of gratitude for the changes in her life.

With joy blooming inside, the music flooded out, filling an unexplainable void. Haley was right. Creativity flowed when an artist was happy. Because of Davis and his two adorable children, Lana was happy for the first time in years. She felt accepted, cared for, appreciated for who she was now instead of being despised for who she used to be.

Above the melody, she heard footsteps on the wooden porch and stopped playing.

The door burst open and there was her heart's desire.

"Davis," she said, elated, leaning her guitar against the hearth as she stood to greet him.

He stalked toward her, his normal smile hidden behind a serious face. "We need to talk."

"Something is wrong." Her good mood disappeared faster than dandelion dust. "What's happened?"

He paced to the hearth, back turned.

"Davis? Tell me. What's wrong? What is it?" She could hear the rising panic in her voice. A few days ago, before she'd let down her guard, she couldn't imagine being this vulnerable. But now, Davis Turner had the power to shatter her into pieces.

"Is it true?" His voice was low, urgent, wounded. "Sydney is not your child?"

The world fell out from under her. She stared at his broad, anvil-shaped back, his sandy hair, the twisted collar of his plaid work shirt and knew in that moment that the dream had ended before it really ever started. She should have told him. She should never have waited.

"Is it?" He spoke softly, still not facing her. The notion hurt like a cinder in the eye. Davis couldn't stand to look at her now.

"I planned to tell you. I wanted to. A thousand times I tried."

He whirled then, the suppressed anger rising to the surface. More devastating than the anger, she saw the hurt. "When? When were you going to tell me that you stole someone else's child and brought her to Whisper Falls where you convinced everyone she was your daughter?"

"I didn't steal her. Sydney is my niece."

That stopped him for several painful heartbeats. "Tess's?"

"Yes." Her insides quivered. Davis knew she'd lied to him, to everyone, and he was furious. "How did you find out?"

"Does it matter?"

"No, no, I suppose it doesn't." She rubbed a hand over her face. "Yes, it does. No one can know. Please, don't say a word to anyone. I don't want Sydney hurt. She's safe here."

"Haven't you already hurt her by taking her away from her mother, from her home?"

She almost laughed, though nothing was funny. They'd had no home.

"I'm protecting her. You have no right to judge my actions when you know nothing about the situation."

"I know you lied to me. You had every chance to tell me about Sydney, but you didn't." He barked a bitter laugh. "You even made up some story about not knowing who the father is. You let me think the worst."

"I told the truth."

"Yeah? Then why not tell me the whole truth? That's what I don't get."

"I was going to."

"When?"

"Soon. When I was sure—"

"Of what? That your house repairs were finished? That I wouldn't turn you in to the police?"

The remark about the house jabbed but she was accustomed to dealing with personal attacks. It was Sydney she worried about.

She held out her hands, pleading. Her fingers shook. "Please, Davis, promise me you won't tell anyone about this. Sydney belongs with me. They'll put her in foster care. I'm her mother in every way but one."

"What about Tess? Doesn't she deserve a say in her daughter's life?"

"She can't take care of Sydney. Never could. Sydney has been with me for years." Even through the ugly times, Sydney had been better off with Lana than Tess. But not a lot.

"Does Tess even know where her daughter is?"

Lana shook her head, knowing how this looked. Her chest tightened, mouth drier than sand. "Telling Tess was too risky."

His mouth twisted sadly. "I can only imagine."

"Tess wasn't a good mother. She had—" She swallowed, ashamed of outing her sister. "Tess has a drug problem."

He didn't seem surprised. "Why not tell the authorities the situation? Why leave Nashville? Why not tell the truth? They'd much rather give custody to a family member than to put in a child in foster care with strangers."

"It wasn't that simple. They would never have let me have custody."

"Why not?"

Lana opened her mouth to admit the ugly reality, but the words wouldn't come. It was bad enough that he believed her a liar and a law-breaker. "I just couldn't risk it."

His jaw tightened. A muscle flexed. Mild-mannered Davis spoke between clenched teeth. "In other words, you won't tell me the truth even now when you have a chance to come clean. What's wrong with you that you can't be honest?"

She gestured absently at the couch, buying time, praying wild prayers for a miracle. "Sit down, Davis. Please. Let's talk."

But he was past listening.

"Talk? So you can tell more lies? So I can be an even bigger fool? What else have you lied about, Lana? Do I dare ask?"

She turned away, afraid. The lid was open to her Pandora's box and she was terribly aware of what could spew forth.

Davis spun her around, holding her by the shoulders. "What are you hiding, Lana? What other things have you kept from me?"

Lana wrapped her arms around her waist and held on tight, shivering. "I don't want you to know. You'll be…disgusted."

He stared down at her, looking her over as if he saw what she was, what she'd been, what she'd always be. His beloved face was close enough to touch and oh, how she wanted to touch him, to plead with him not to hate her. She dropped her head, too ashamed to meet his stormy eyes.

"Tell me, Lana. You owe me that much. What are you hiding?"

She swallowed a thick wad of despair. Nothing mattered now. Whether she told him or not, he was gone. She could hear it in his voice. They were over.

She threw her head back and blurted the words to the ceiling. "I'm a drunk, Davis. An alcoholic. I spent time in jail, in back alleys and a lot of other places I can't remember. I'd do anything to get blitzed. Anything." She glared at him, sick with fury at having to remember. "Don't you get it? I couldn't even sing unless I was stoned out of my mind. Even after I gave my life to Jesus, with a record like that, no one was going to let me raise a child."

His face had paled as she spoke. He dropped his hands to his sides and stood, like a defeated boxer, spent.

His terrible, dark silence broke her. A tear seeped and slowly slid down her face. Tension vibrated in the room, thick enough to make her shudder.

In a low and wounded voice, Davis said, "You should have told me."

"Would you have understood if I had?"

"I don't know. I would have tried. You never gave me the chance." He paced to the window, a pane he'd put in himself and looked outside on the yard he'd helped her clean. "Tell me this much, Lana."

His voice was soft, wounded. "Were you using me, the way Jenny said, to get your house remodeled?"

"No!" An aching chasm widened in her chest, dark and bottomless. If she fell into that black hole again, she'd be lost forever. "You can't believe that—"

"People tried to warn me, but you had me fooled. I thought you'd changed. I believed you were the pious woman you claimed to be. I believed you cared about me and my kids."

"I do. I do." She moved toward him, hands outstretched.

He backed away, shaking his head. "I cared about you, Lana. For the first time since Cheryl died, I thought I'd found a woman who matched me, someone I could love and build a life with. But you're not who I thought you were. Not even close."

With that searing judgment, he spun on the heel of his work boots and stormed out of her house. She followed him to the door, one hand on her mouth to stop the cries of despair, the other holding her churning stomach.

She watched him jog across the street and down the block. She watched until he disappeared into the pretty, buff brick house. A few hundred feet might as well be a million miles.

"Lana?"

Lana lay on the couch, one arm thrown across

her eyes when she heard Sydney's footsteps on the stairs.

"What?" she mumbled, wishing she didn't have to talk to anyone right this minute, not even the child she would sacrifice anything for. As much as Lana anguished over losing Davis, she'd lie again to protect this precious little girl.

"Davis was really mad, wasn't he?"

Her heart sank. Sydney had been upstairs doing a school project on the laptop. Lana had prayed the child hadn't heard the argument. Lately, she was batting zero on answered prayers.

"I'm sorry you heard that."

"Why is he so mad? Is it because of me? He's mad because I'm not your real daughter."

Hearing the anxiety and hurt in Sydney's voice, Lana sat up. "No, sugar. Davis is not mad at you."

"I thought he liked me."

"He does. He adores you." She pulled Sydney onto her lap with a heavy sigh. "What's not to like? One smart, beautiful, well-behaved girl with the prettiest eyes and the brightest smile in the world. Anyone would love you, Sydney."

"Not my mom."

The load was impossible. No one should have to explain to a nine-year-old the facts of a drug-addicted life. "Tess loves you, baby. She's too sick to take care of you."

"She's not sick. She takes drugs. We learned at school about bad drugs, Lana. My mom takes them.

The kind with the spoons and the needles. I saw her. And then she'd be all weird and scary."

"I know. I know." Lana buried her face in Sydney's hair. "That's why she gave you to me. She knew she wasn't good for you and she loved you enough to let you go. That took courage on her part." And Lana threatening to turn her in.

"Really?"

"Yes." She folded Sydney into her lap and rocked, humming softly the way she'd done so many times when the girl was small.

"Lana?"

Lana stopped humming. "What, baby?"

"Davis isn't going to be my daddy, is he?"

The question crushed her. This is the way it would always be. She and Sydney against the world, alone and wishing for the impossible. No one in Whisper Falls would ever believe Lana was a new creature in Christ. She didn't even believe it herself. She'd always be one of those "awful Ross girls."

Maybe they should move again. Somewhere.

Chapter Fourteen

Davis finally found time to do the remodel work for Austin and Annalisa, but it wasn't going well. Not well at all.

With a grunt, he jammed a freshly cut diamond of tile into place above the sink. Frustrated that it was a fraction too large, he pushed harder. The expensive tile snapped.

He grabbed the fragments and threw them as hard as he could. The sound banged against the wall and clattered to the floor.

"Rough day?" Austin Blackwell's voice turned him around.

He felt as Nathan must have when Davis caught him drawing happy faces on his bedroom wall. "I thought you were moving cattle."

"Moved 'em." The big cowboy leaned a shoulder against the doorjamb. "Everything all right with you?"

"Yeah." Davis stacked his hands on his hips and

dropped his head. Pieces of tile sparkled in the artificial light at his feet. He'd never done that before. Not even in the frustrating days of training. "No."

"That's what I figured. You're not yourself the past couple of days." Austin jerked his head toward the hallway. "Coffee's on."

"Thanks." Davis followed the other man down the hall and into the kitchen, feeling awkward but wanting to explain. Somehow. "Look, Austin, I apologize for what just happened. I don't want you to think this has anything to do with your tile job. I'll get this fixed up nice for Annalisa before Christmas the way you want. I want to. It's just that…I've got…stuff on my mind."

"I figured. You're not a person to throw things and have fits." The tall cowboy pointed a coffee mug and grinned. "That would be my sister."

Davis returned the grin as he scraped back a chair and sat down at the wooden table. Austin put the cup of coffee in front him and sat down with his own.

"I don't make a habit of sticking my face in another man's business but if you want to talk…"

The statement almost made Davis laugh. Austin was about as private as a man could get, a man who didn't carry tales, a man to trust.

"I'm a mess."

"Must be a woman."

Davis huffed out a frustrated breath. "Yeah."

"Been there."

Yes, he had, though Davis didn't know all the details. Right now, he hurt so bad, he couldn't sleep, couldn't think straight and, apparently, couldn't even do his job well—the work he loved, the work Lana referred to as his art.

He felt torn between what he wanted and what he thought was the right thing to do. His first priority was his children, but all Nathan and Paige had done since the big reveal was mope around or ask to go to Lana's house. Even the coming Christmas parade and bazaar didn't excite them. They wanted Lana and Sydney to come along, and even his best explanation wasn't good enough. As disappointed as he was with Lana, he'd never tell his kids about her lifestyle.

"Lana," he said.

"Figured as much. You two seemed pretty tight. Annalisa predicted wedding bells."

The comment shot a knife through his gut. "Not hardly." And then, like a compressed volcano, the words flowed out. There in the Blackwells' kitchen with an old black dog at his feet and a coffee cup in hand, he opened his soul to a good friend. Austin reacted as expected. He sipped his coffee and listened.

When the words ran out, the room grew silent except for the occasional tick of a digital clock and the soft snore of the old dog.

Austin pushed back from the table to refill the coffee cups. Davis shook his head. He'd barely

touched his. A fuzzy poodle with red painted toe-
nails tapped into the kitchen and laid her head on
the lab. The old dog sighed as if he'd been expecting the interruption.

"What are you going to do?"

"I don't know." Davis stuck his elbows on the
table and clasped his hands. "Nothing, I suppose,
though I worry about Sydney, Lana's little—" He
caught himself. "The little girl."

"Why? Does Lana mistreat her?"

"Lana? No way! Lana's a great mother. She's
crazy about that kid. She sacrificed everything to
bring Sydney here and give her a good home."

Austin studied him for a long, silent moment.
"Sounds like you still care. Are you going to turn
her in?"

"No. No." The idea of pulling Sydney away from
the woman she considered her mother was impossible. "I can't. Maybe I should but I can't. I'm not
sure what to do. I wish Lana had been straight with
me from the beginning."

"Secrets hurt."

"Tell me about it. I thought we had something. I
knew she hadn't led a perfect life and she knew that
I knew. So why couldn't she trust me with the rest?"

Austin was quiet again for a few seconds. Then,
he set his coffee aside and leaned forward. "When
my first wife died, I was accused of her murder.
You probably know that."

Davis nodded. He'd heard. He also knew the cowboy was found innocent.

"You can't imagine the pain and shame that comes with a charge of that magnitude. And the grief. I was out of my mind with it. I moved here, kept to myself, afraid my secret would get out." Austin huffed softly. "Afraid of what people would think and of how they'd stare at me and wonder if I'd kill them, too. That's a hard thing to bear, Davis."

"But you were innocent." Lana wasn't, and Davis didn't see how the two situations compared.

"Yes. But keeping that secret almost cost me a chance at a life with Annalisa." Austin swigged his coffee and stood. "Only got one other thing to say, Davis. A man knows his own heart and you gotta do what's right for you and your family. But remember this, too. It's carried me through some tough times. *Whom the Son has set free is free indeed.*"

While Davis pondered the Bible verse, Austin jammed his hat on his dark head. "I gotta get back to work. I suspect you do, too. Don't bother to lock up when you leave. I'll be in the barn."

He nodded once and went out the back door.

The poodle hopped up to follow, then changed her mind and tagged along with Davis. He went back to the broken tile, his mind trying to unravel the conversation with Austin. What exactly was his friend getting at?

After another frustrating hour of mismeasuring,

broken tile and questioning looks from a prissy poodle, Davis tossed his tools into his truck and headed toward Jenny's house. Getting over Lana was going to take more than a conversation and a cup of hot coffee.

As he drove through town, he spotted her coming out of the newspaper office. His heart leaped and then sank like the *Titanic*. She looked great, her mink hair flowing over her shoulders, a bright blue scarf around her neck. Sydney was with her. The little girl pointed at something and smiled her shy smile. Davis suffered an undeniable pull toward the woman and child. Would she even speak to him if he stopped? He tapped the brake and then thought better of it.

Leave it alone. Let her go. Trust is crucial in a relationship.

He wished she'd told him. He liked to think he would have been man enough to weather the storm.

Even after he drove on, he watched Lana and Sydney in the rearview mirror until, holding hands they went inside the dollar store.

Tomorrow was the Christmas bazaar, a massive event that took place inside the community center. She'd be there, gathering the news for the paper. He'd be there, too, as promised, helping with setup, teardown and anything else Miss Evelyn needed. Along with most other business people, he'd donated to the cause. This year, he'd upped his donation, hoping for larger bids that would help Jenny and Chuck gather the finances they needed for Charlie's surgery. Not that they didn't have insurance, but insurance didn't cover everything. Not even close. For people from remote areas, just the cost of staying away from home for long stretches of time was burdensome. Add transportation, co-pays, deductibles and all the extras, and average folk were strapped.

At Jenny's house, he said hello to Charlie before collecting his children. The boy was on oxygen now most of the time, his lips blue and his energy low. He'd gone downhill rapidly.

"The cardiologist thinks we can wait until after the New Year to have the surgery." Jenny twisted her hands, a perpetual stress line between her eyes. "Chuck isn't sure that's the right thing to do."

"He's scared, sis."

"I know. I am, too. But the doctor gave me his personal number in case something goes wrong. I trust him."

"That's good." He shifted, worried, wanting to help and not knowing how. "Are Nathan and Paige too much right now? I can ask Mom to watch them."

"Of course not. Unless you don't want them staying with me anymore." She put a hand to her mouth. "You're still mad at me, aren't you?"

"No." He wasn't mad, he was broken.

"I can't bear it if you are. With all of this—" Her hand fluttered but he understood. She was on overload, afraid for her child, working on town and church events, preparing for Christmas while caring for a husband and kids, including his.

"You did what you did out of love. I get that." Davis pulled her into a hug, heavy-hearted. When he released her, he said, "See you tomorrow?"

"Wouldn't miss it. Charlie's excited about going."

"Come on, munchkins," he called to his kids and led the way to the truck.

On the short drive home, Paige and Nathan were unusually subdued. They weren't even playing a video game. He knew something was up.

"Daddy," Paige said, as they drove past the glistening river. "Is Charlie going to die?"

Davis flinched. He didn't normally balk at discussing anything with his kids, but this was a tough one. He made his voice sound especially chipper. "Charlie is going to get an operation. If all goes well, he'll be jumping on the trampoline pretty soon and by summer, you can all go swimming together."

"But he could die. Like Mommy."

Davis gripped the steering wheel tighter. So much for being chipper. "No one can answer that for sure, pumpkin, but we will pray every day that Charlie gets well."

"Can we pray for Lana, too? She's sad that you're mad at her."

"I'm not mad—" He shot a look in the mirror. "How do you know she's sad?"

"Sydney told me at school. She said they might

move away again and she's scared she'll have to go to foster care."

Move away? Where?

"That's not going to happen." As if he had any say in either matter.

"Can we go see them after dinner?" Nathan asked. "I made Lana a present in art class."

"That's not a good idea, buddy."

"Why? Sydney said they bought us a present. She said they miss us something awful. I miss them something awful, too. Can't you kiss and make up?"

"I don't think so, pal."

"Don't you love her anymore?"

There was the crux. He did. His kids did. Nothing she'd told him had changed that.

He stopped the truck in the driveway and sat at the wheel looking up the street at the Ross house. He had no words to explain the complicated issue to his children. He couldn't even explain it to himself. Even if he could, their thinking was different. They saw with their hearts. They lived in the here and now, heedless of past mistakes, believing in the person Lana appeared to be. She'd been good to them. She'd loved them and they'd loved her in return. That's all they understood.

Why couldn't adulthood could be that simple?

The Whisper Falls Community Center was packed. An all-purpose building, the floor had been covered and now boasted long tables and booths laden with Christmas arts and crafts, silent auction items and tons of beautiful food and colorful gift baskets. At one end, a stage had been set up for entertainment and announcements.

Lana moved around the large open area, Sydney at her side, admiring the handiwork of many artists and crafters. Even her best attempts at making Christmas ornaments with Haley were laughable compared to the blown glass, the leatherwork, the gorgeous woodworking. She was glad she'd left her childish attempts at home. Haley's art, on the other hand, was proving popular. Her auburn-haired friend's table was surrounded by customers snatching up whimsical birdhouses and elegantly carved vases. All the while, Haley painted, personalizing the artwork on request. She was in her element with a proud husband at her side, talking to customers in his charming way.

"Donations are off the charts this year," Miss Evelyn said as she bustled past, an iPad in hand. "Look at all these out-of-towners. You're going to sing for us later, aren't you?"

Lana's heart jumped into her throat. They'd hired a band. They didn't need her. Someone called Evelyn's name and she rushed away, leaving Lana to wonder why the older woman kept pushing.

Across the gym she saw Davis and the children arrive along with Jenny and Chuck. Chuck pushed a wan, listless Charlie in a wheelchair, a heartbreaking sight. Little boys were supposed to be full of energy like Nathan. Her gaze went to the dimple-cheeked boy who'd stolen her heart. She missed his hugs, his sweetness, his funny, little-boy view of the world.

Davis caught her looking and leveled a steady, heart-thudding stare in return. She glanced away.

Apparently, he'd kept her secret, though he'd never promised. She'd worried about that, afraid she'd have to take Sydney and run again. She'd do it if she had to, just as any mother would do what was right for her child. But Sydney was happy here. She was doing better in school. She'd made friends. Even though she missed the Davis children, Sydney was excited about Christmas. Lana was determined to give her the best one of her life.

"There's a lot to see," she said as the Boggy Boys Band struck up a bluegrass tune. "Do you want your face painted?"

"Can I ask Paige to come with me?"

"I don't think so, sugar." She'd known they would run into the Davis trio, but she couldn't let that stop her from doing her part for the event. In a town as small as Whisper Falls, seeing the Turner family was inevitable. They'd have to cope and move on. Somehow.

"I signed up to help with the concession. Want some barbecue?"

"I guess."

Lana poked a finger in Sydney's ribs. "Don't be so enthusiastic."

They made their way through a sea of people to the concession area, drawn by the smell of donated barbecued ribs and all the fixings. Lana got busy filling foam plates with baked beans while Cassie Blackwell added the potato salad. Uninterested in food, Sydney moped for a few minutes until a girl from her class whisked her off to the face painting.

"Great crowd," Cassie said. "I'm really glad. The more money we make, the more we can donate to Charlie's fund."

Cassie was one of those irrepressible personalities that everyone liked. Pretty in a long, sparkly Christmas sweater, black tights and very high heels, her white skin was accented by straight black hair and bright red lipstick. She loved to talk and was even better at listening.

"Here girls, put on your Santa hats." The speaker, an older woman she recognized as Creed Carter's mother, handed out the red-and-white caps. Lana tried to get into the festive mood though her heart wasn't in it. How could it be, when her heart was across the room? Try as she might, she couldn't stop watching for him. He was working, too, carrying boxes to the various tables to keep the merchants stocked.

For the thousandth time she wished she'd trusted him from the beginning. He'd always been a stand-up guy—a fact that brought her full circle. Davis deserved better. The breakup was for the best.

But he'd said he cared for her, and dreams die hard.

She missed him something awful, missed the evenings with him and his children, missed the conversations, the laughter, the kisses.

"Hi, Lana."

The small voice pulled her focus away from Davis to his children standing on the opposite side of the serving counter. Paige and Nathan, money in hand, had joined the line of diners.

"Hi, you two. Want some barbecue?" She tried to be as casual as possible, but she wanted to run around the end of the counter and scoop them up.

"Three rib dinners, please," Paige said. "But I don't want any potato salad."

"No potato salad. Coming right up."

She fixed the plates and handed them over, adding an extra couple of ribs to Davis's order. A meat and potato man, he loved barbecue, as she'd learned the day they'd ripped out the kitchen's ancient, decayed paneling. He'd purposely ordered enough barbecue ribs to last the weekend. They'd giggled like kids over the messy sauce, the pile of red-stained paper towels and the hot, hot sauce he'd convinced her to try. Her tongue still burned at the memory.

Paige leaned in closer. "Daddy said to tell you hi."

She doubted that very much. "That's really nice of him."

"Should I tell him hi for you?" The child's face was so eager, Lana couldn't let her down.

"That would be nice."

The pair exchanged a conspiratorial glance as they left. Lana shook her head. Such good kids. As they walked away, Lana saw that Paige's red hair bow matched Sydney's, a purchase they'd made together. "Like sisters," they'd said proudly.

I love you. You love me. Let's be sisters. If only life was that simple.

"Why don't you knock off a while and eat with them?" Cassie pointed a ladle at the pair weaving their way through the crowd and toward their father.

"Better not. Davis is not speaking to me at the moment."

"Could have fooled me. I'm watching you watch him. And he's watching you when you aren't watching him."

Lana snorted. "Can you repeat that?"

Cassie laughed and stuck out her tongue. "Not a chance. Just go. Make both of you happy."

But Lana didn't. The community center grew more crowded by the moment and her line was long and getting longer. Bluegrass music shifted to country and she found herself humming to the familiar tunes as she dipped the steaming beans. No one seemed to mind that their server was one of those Ross girls.

After a while, the band took a break and Miss Evelyn made announcements, reminding everyone to sign up for the silent auction. A man Lana didn't recognize moved close to the stage and handed Miss Evelyn a note. She read it silently and then stuck the paper in her pocket. Then she completed her announcements and left the stage with her usual bustling energy. Lana didn't see her again until she appeared at the concession.

"Lana, honey, we need to talk." Miss Evelyn motioned to a bald man in the line. "Cecil, take Lana's spot for a few minutes, will you? As a favor to me? Come see me on Monday for a slice of hot apple pie. On the house."

Cecil looked a little surprised but good-naturedly did as she requested. That was the power of Evelyn Parsons.

Lana was surprised, too. What could Miss Evelyn possibly want to say that couldn't wait?

She followed the bustling, curly haired dynamo to a quiet corner—the quietest place they could find in the jam-packed building.

"Is something wrong?" Lana glanced around for Sydney. Spotting her with a friend, she relaxed.

Miss Evelyn pulled a rumpled piece of paper from her skirt pocket. "A man has offered a large sum of money to Charlie's fund."

"That's fantastic!"

"I thought so, too. All he wants in exchange is to hear you sing."

Lana blinked. Her brain went numb. "What?"

"He requested this specific song." Evelyn pushed the paper into Lana's hands. "Do you know it?"

With trembling fingers, Lana smoothed the note and read the song title. In a shocked whisper, she said, "Yes, I do. I wrote this song."

"Well, how about that!" Miss Evelyn exclaimed, clearly more pleased than Lana. "This could not be more perfect. The town can enjoy your fabulous gift and Charlie's fund gets a fat boost."

"No, I can't, Miss Evelyn, I can't. Don't ask me to sing. I'll do anything else, but not that."

The older woman took both of Lana's hands in hers, crumpling the paper between them. "Lana, I've known you since you were a sad little girl trying to deal with that troubled mother of yours. Every time you came into the Iron Horse with your sister, I'd think, 'That child is special.'"

"You were always kind to us." Emotion pushed up inside Lana's chest. Evelyn and Digger had let the twins hang out at the Iron Horse many days when going home was too hard. Free food and a kind word had made a difference. "I remember when you tried to help Mama."

"Actually I was trying to help you girls. Your mama didn't want help. Called me an old biddy and told me to mind my own business." Miss

Evelyn chuckled as if the insult was funny. "But you girls—well, I regret not doing more. I knew things were bad after your daddy left and Patricia was so bitter."

"Daddy couldn't take it anymore."

"He shouldn't have left you girls to deal with her. Looking back I think she might have been sick. But that didn't help you and Tess. You had it rough, but look at you now. Doing great, raising that precious Sydney. And writing songs like this. God gave you a magnificent gift."

Lana shook her head. "Not so magnificent, Miss Evelyn. I can't sing in public anymore."

"Not even for a sick child?" The disappointment on Evelyn's face hurt. "Why, honey?"

Lana wanted to sing, but she couldn't. She'd freeze up and fall apart. She'd make a fool of herself.

"Something happened. I had to stop." Evelyn's questioning eyes bore into her until she finally whispered, "I gave my life to Christ. I stopped drinking."

"That's a good thing, Lana, but I don't see what it has to do with singing that song." She dropped her hold on Lana's hands and tapped the paper.

Quietly, painfully, Lana told her. Hiding the truth had already cost her one friend. "A bottle of gin was my courage. I can't go on stage without it."

Evelyn's eyes searched hers, piercing as if she could see inside. She took Lana's face between her soft, lotion-scented hands and leaned close. "Lana, honey. Don't you know who you are?"

Lana shook her head. Of course, she knew. She was one of those awful Ross girls. She was a loser, a failure.

But Miss Evelyn held her in a fast grip, forcing her to listen. "You are a child of the Most High God. You can do anything He says you can do. God is your strength. You don't need gin or anything else." Evelyn pointed toward Charlie. "But that little boy over there in the wheelchair needs something and you can help him get it."

All she had to do was go on stage and fall apart in front of the entire town. If she wasn't already the least liked person in Whisper Falls, she would be then.

But there was Charlie, Davis's nephew.

Torn, struggling, longing to help but afraid, Lana looked again at the sheet of paper. As she read the song title, Lana was suddenly aware of a startling fact. She'd never submitted that song anywhere. "How does this man know me? Where did he get this?"

Miss Evelyn looked baffled. "He didn't say. I suppose wherever songwriters send their music to be published."

"I didn't. No one has a copy of this except—" Davis. A shock ran through her like electricity. Davis didn't have this kind of money. "Is Davis Turner the donor?"

"Davis? No. The man's name is on the back. Perry Grider."

Lana turned the paper over and read the dark scrawl. Who was this guy? "I don't know him."

"Neither do I, but he had cash in hand, Lana. This is for real."

Cash in hand. A large donation for Charlie's fund. All in exchange for a three-minute song.

"Let me think a minute, okay?" Think and pray and throw up a while.

"Don't take too long. We got a live one. We don't want him to get away." Evelyn chortled at her own joke before growing serious again. "Remember, honey, your gift is your music. God gave you that. If your gift can help someone, He expects you to use it. He'll carry you through. Remember who you are."

Already starting to hyperventilate, Lana nodded numbly. "Okay. Okay."

Then she rushed to the restroom and locked herself inside a stall. This was crazy. Weird and incomprehensible. A thousand thoughts ran through her head. Fear of getting on that stage. Evelyn's strange comments. Charlie's need for surgery. Curiosity about the stranger. Who was he and why would he pay to hear her sing her own song?

She closed her eyes tight. She couldn't get on that stage.

What if it was Sydney? The thought flashed

through her head like a Las Vegas marquee. What if her precious girl needed an expensive operation?

She took a deep, shaky breath and prayed. Miss Evelyn's words came back to her. *Don't you know who you are?* You're not Lana Ross, the drunk party girl. You're Lana Ross, child of the Most High, cleansed by a sacrifice far greater than singing in front of hundreds of people.

Her strength was in God. Not a bottle of gin. Her gift was her music. A God gift. Hadn't Davis said the same thing? If she could use her gift to help a child, shouldn't she try?

So what if she failed? She'd been humiliated before. She had to make the effort.

Knees shaking, she straightened her shoulders and headed out of the restroom and across the floor. She passed Davis and Jenny and Chuck and with more courage than she thought she had, she stopped to say hello to Charlie whose sick, little-boy smile encouraged her to keep going. He reminded her so much of Nathan.

Davis's gaze snagged hers, and he started to say something. She touched his arm and went on. Her heart hammered louder than the drums.

When she approached the stage Miss Evelyn saw her and lifted her eyebrows in question.

"I need to borrow a guitar." Jitters raced up her spine and quivered in her voice.

Evelyn did a mini fist pump. "That's our girl. I knew you wouldn't let us down."

Don't be so sure. I still might run like a rabbit on amphetamines.

Fighting down the butterflies, swallowing the threat of sickness, Lana moved to the edge of the stage while Miss Evelyn approached the microphone. The band stopped playing. The noise in the building continued, the voices and the shuffling feet. Doors opened, paper crinkled.

Help me, Lord Jesus. I can't do this by myself. I don't know if I can do it at all. I am Your child. I am Your child.

She'd no more than whispered the prayer than she spotted Davis, slowly pushing Charlie's wheelchair closer to the stage. His eyes were on her, questioning, though she didn't know the reason.

She looked at the little boy in the chair, focused on him instead of the violent shaking inside. "Not for me. For Charlie."

She heard Miss Evelyn's voice making the announcement, but her ears roared so loud she comprehended nothing other than her name. A gasp rose from the audience and then applause. All eyes, not just Davis's, were on her.

A band member held out an electric acoustic.

What if she bolted? What if she couldn't do this? What if she failed?

The old need for a drink roared in, vicious and clawing. One drink. Just one to stop the shakes. To loosen up the dry vocal cords.

Don't you know who you are?

Lana gripped the neck of the guitar and nodded her thanks. Slipping the strap over her shoulder felt natural, second nature. She tested the strings, found them well-tuned, though her fingers felt numb and cold.

Throat drier than Arizona, breath short, she stepped to the mike. She cleared her throat, buying time, wondering if her heart was going to fly out of her chest or if her knees would buckle.

The audience waited, quieter now.

She strummed the strings, found the melody in her head and began to fingerpick the intro. She played it once, twice, praying the words would come.

The wild urge to run made her legs wobbly.

Her eyes found Charlie and the man behind him. Davis smiled at her. Like a drowning soul, she clung to the life raft in his eyes. He gave one encouraging nod and mouthed something.

What did he say? She frowned at him in question, aware that her fingers were moving and the audience waited in expectation.

As his mouth moved again, Davis tapped a fist over his heart, and then he pointed at Lana with a nod.

And Lana began to sing.

Goose bumps raced up and down Davis's spine. He recognized that song. His song. The one she'd given him. The one he'd— Unfettered delight exploded in his chest. He jerked his head right and left, quickly scanning the packed crowd for Joshua Kendle. Did he know? Was he here?

"On wings of the wind, through clouds and the rain, your love carries me, carries me."

The lyrics drew him back to Lana. The other would take care of itself. For now, he wanted nothing more than to watch a miracle unfold.

She was as pale as a sheet, but the rough honey vocals were perfection. Like a tile mosaic of intricate design, emotion flowed from her lips and fingers. At first her eyes were closed but she'd opened them and found him. He held on, willing her to stand strong. She could do this. He knew she could.

He saw her knees shake, her fingers tremble and once in a while her lips quivered. He knew how scared she was. But while her body quaked, beauty and emotion flowed from her throat.

"You got this," he murmured, encouraging her in every way possible from ten feet away. "I'm sorry. Thank you. You're awesome."

He muttered a litany of apologies and random thoughts, more grateful than he could ever say for her sacrifice.

Miss Evelyn's announcement had nearly taken him to his knees. Even Jenny had begun to weep. Though Lana had not sung in public for a long time, someone was donating to Charlie's fund in exchange for a song. So she had agreed.

He knew the fear that haunted her. He knew how

hard this was. She was terrified and yet, she had agreed for Charlie. His nephew. For the child of a woman who'd given her nothing but grief.

Why had he been such a coldhearted, selfish idiot? Lana would always put a child's needs before her own. Sydney's and now Charlie's.

Suddenly he understood what Austin had been trying to tell him. Lana's mistakes, like his and everyone else's, had been nailed to a cross. The moment she accepted Him, she was free of her past. She might still be working through some areas, trying to find her way, but who wasn't?

She was a good and decent person. And he loved her. He'd been miserable without her. He'd known all along she made him better, that she was the missing piece of his life, but he had allowed pride and opinion to rob them both.

She had every reason not to forgive him, but he prayed she would.

As Lana kicked into the final chorus, Davis turned to Jenny. "She did this for Charlie. Lana has paralyzing stage fright but she went up there for *your son*."

Tears gathered in his sister's eyes. "I don't know what to say."

"Say you were wrong. I was, too. I love her, Jenny, and I'm going to tell her even if she kicks me to the curb." Leaving his weeping sister, he excused his way through the crowd that now pressed against the stage. He approached the steps at one end, counting on her to exit the direction she'd entered.

The song ended and the building erupted in applause and cheers. Lana remained at the microphone, guitar against her body, with a bewildered expression as if she couldn't believe the applause was for her. Someone whistled a loud *whoot*. On the opposite side of the stage, Miss Evelyn practically levitated with excitement.

Davis started up the steps, not wanting to steal Lana's moment but eager to hold her in his arms, to apologize. If she'd let him.

Then Lana smiled—a wide, relieved smile—handed the guitar to its owner and took a quick bow. As she turned to exit the stage she saw him and froze.

Davis paused, adrenaline jacked, feeling a bit trembly himself. "You were phenomenal."

She took a step toward him. "I was scared to death."

"That's what made it phenomenal. You were afraid, but you sang. For Charlie."

She took another step. And then another.

The crowd of people faded into the background. Sound ceased. Davis saw and heard nothing but the special woman he'd almost thrown away.

"I've been an idiot," he said. "Forgive me? *Please* forgive me."

She didn't hesitate. Faster than he could breathe, Lana was in his embrace.

"I was wrong not to tell you," she said. "You had every right to despise me. I've made too many mistakes."

He stroked her soft hair. "Shh. Shh. I don't despise you. I never could. You're amazing. I was the one out of line."

The calloused tips of her fingers rubbed lovingly across his jaw. "I missed you so much."

"I was such a jerk. You should make this harder on me. Make me grovel." He looped a lock of hair behind her ear. "Do you know how many times I've had to stop myself from coming to your house?"

"Me, too. I'd look out the window and see you or the kids coming or going and I wanted to run to you."

"Can we start fresh? Start new? Try again?"

"Are you sure you can forget what I've done and where I've been? I don't want to hold you back or make you or the kids ashamed to know me."

"You could never do that. I'm proud of you, Lana. *Proud.*" He cupped her face, more grateful than he could ever express. She'd forgiven him. Just like that. "Can you forget the ugly things I said?"

"I already have."

"There we are then. Forgotten. Forgiven." *Whom the Son has set free is free indeed.* Austin Blackwell was a wise man. "Lana Ross," he said. "You are an amazing, gifted child of God, a loving mother, a good friend, the woman who holds my heart. I want you in my life. Say you want me, too."

"Oh, I do. So much." Lana pressed her cheek against Davis's chest. "I feel like I'm dreaming."

He cupped the back of her head, aware of her warm breath seeping through his shirt. "If you are, don't wake up. I like it here."

"Daddy?" a small voice said.

Davis let his head drop against her hair. "Uh-oh. The dream is over."

Lana laughed softly and took a step away. Her absence left a cold spot. He caught her hand and tugged her back, sliding a possessive arm around her. No matter what anyone thought or said, he wasn't letting go this time. Let the whole world know for all he cared.

"Daddy." Nathan squinted up at them, expression intense. "Does this mean you and Lana are in love again?"

The adults exchanged looks. What Davis saw in Lana's eyes was all the answer he needed.

"Yes, son. I think it does."

Chapter Fifteen

The Christmas Bazaar was in a word, bizarre. Good bizarre.

Too astonished and happy to do anything but grin, Lana held Davis's hand in a near death grip as they walked through the exhibits in search of the man who'd paid such a high price for a song. Her knees still shook but for a different reason now. It was as if the earth had moved and the world had suddenly righted itself. A world that had never made sense finally did.

Love was a powerful thing. She prayed with all her heart that this would last. That Davis wouldn't change his mind again and that she would have the courage to keep believing.

In front of them, Sydney, Paige and Nathan hopped and giggled and whirled in circles like wind-up Christmas toys, making a path through the well-wishers. With each step, someone stopped her to compliment her music, to ask when she would sing again, to invite her to events.

The terror had come, but she'd won. She and God. With the help of a very special man.

"I didn't fall down," she whispered as they walked past a display of wood-carved clocks.

Davis smiled his thousand-watt smile. "I would never let you fall."

That was part of the wonder, the knowledge that somehow the finest man on earth had seen past her faults and loved her anyway.

The same way Jesus had.

"Lana." A female voice turned her around. Jenny stood there, a determined expression on her face.

Lana stiffened, sucked in a breath and waited for the subtle digs or outright hostility. Coming off the high of singing again, she didn't want this confrontation, but she wouldn't run away from it either. Jenny had reason to dislike her but it was time for both of them to grow up and move on.

Not wanting to put Davis in the middle, Lana removed her hand from his.

Wonder of wonders, Davis shifted closer and put his strong workman's arm around her waist, securing her to his side, supporting her.

"Hi, sis," he said to Jenny.

Twisting her fingers, Jenny barely nodded to her brother. Her focus was on Lana. Instead of the expected hostility, Lana saw sadness.

"Your song…Miss Evelyn said…" Jenny's eyes

dropped shut. Tears slid from beneath each lid. "Thank you for what you did."

"I hope Charlie's operation makes him well. That's all that matters."

Jenny smiled a wobbly, watery smile and walked away.

"You let her off easy," Davis said. "I love you for that. She's my sister, a good woman, but lately—" He shook his head, palms up in a gesture of helplessness.

"She's a scared mother. No matter what happened before, Charlie's situation takes center stage. I feel sorry for what Jenny's going through."

"See? Amazing. Generous. Good to the core." He snagged her hand again and looked around. "Now where is that Perry guy?"

"I can't imagine what that was all about. He knew about my song, Davis, the one I shared with you."

"We'll find out, don't worry," Davis said with an odd twinkle in his eyes.

But they didn't. Regardless of their search and even after speaking with Miss Evelyn, they never found him. For some baffling reasons, a stranger named Perry Grider had come in, requested the song, left a large chunk of money and disappeared without another word.

Finally, Lana said, "I have to get back to the serving line." She didn't want to. She wanted to stay right beside Davis and enjoy the pure freedom the night had brought. "I promised."

"I hear you. I have some things to do, too." He leaned in to kiss her forehead. "You smell really good."

Lana wrinkled her nose. "Like barbecue?"

"Hey, nothing wrong with that. Love that smell. Very romantic."

She laughed. "I'll remember that."

They stood smiling at each other like two lunatics, knowing they had to separate but reluctant.

"Later?" Davis asked.

"Absolutely."

The rest of the evening flew by in a happy blur of dishing up beans while catching glimpses of Davis. She saw him everywhere helping out. He even talked to Joshua Kendle for a while, apparently about something that made them both happy. They exchanged high fives and slapped each other on the back. During the exchange he glanced her way and grinned. Her silly pulse had gone off the charts.

The three little matchmakers popped by a couple of times to be sure the five of them would have some togetherness before the day ended.

"Daddy says come to our house after," Nathan insisted. "We have mistletoe."

Chuckling at the pure cuteness, Lana stopped serving long enough to grab a hug. "How can I turn that down?"

Back with the baked beans, she watched them skip away, giggling and excited. They were such loves, all three of them.

"Great event, huh?" Cassie asked suggestively as she twitched her perfectly arched eyebrows.

"Can't argue with that." The only imperfection was the mystery she hadn't solved. Who was Perry Grider and how did he know about her song?

The days leading up to Christmas were the happiest of Lana's life. She was loved by a wonderful man and the association with Davis brought her a new respectability. At least, she assumed that was the reason she no longer felt like an outcast in Whisper Falls.

She and Sydney, usually with Davis, Nathan and Paige along, attended a whirlwind of Christmas events—everything from church plays, caroling and cantatas to the adorable musical program at Sydney's school. As her writing skills improved, the articles came faster and easier, and she found more time for her music and for working on the house with Davis. The latter, when they could talk and unwind together, was the best part of her day.

With Davis's support, she'd gathered the courage to file for Sydney's guardianship. Guided by Haley and Creed, who had gone through a similar situation with Rose and knew the ropes, the process wasn't nearly as bad as Lana had expected. Even with her past, the social worker had been confident that two years of sobriety and a town filled with references would do the trick. Lana's eyes filled with grateful tears every time she thought about all the good things that had happened to her in Whisper Falls.

Yesterday with enthusiastic help from the three children, she'd created "gifts in a jar" for teachers and friends, the pastor, her boss and others. Then, today, Christmas Eve, the trio made the rounds, ho-ho-ho-ing and singing "Jingle Bells" at the top of their lungs as they delivered the goodies while Davis put the final touches on Annalisa Blackwell's tile work.

Davis was picking up something afterward, though the children had no idea she and Davis had found exactly the right puppy to put under Sydney's tree. Why not? They were here for good. Whisper Falls was finally home.

Steps light, she guided the children across the street, listening to their excited chatter. Her Sydney seemed so much happier and more secure these days. Lana giggled inside, anticipating the child's joy when she met the fat ball of love.

At the newspaper office, Joshua Kendle gave her a "little something" in an envelope, her first bonus ever, and requested all the articles she had time to write. She threw her arms around his neck and hugged him. Then embarrassed, she stepped away only to find him laughing at her.

"You folks have a merry Christmas," he said. "And tell Davis not to worry. I'll be happy whatever you decide."

Lana stopped in the doorway. "What?"

"Never mind. You'll know soon enough. And you don't even have to thank me." When she frowned in bewilderment, he waved her off. "Merry Christmas, now."

Then he turned back to his computer and left her to wonder.

"I'm a little nervous," Lana said that evening as the five of them drove toward Davis's parents' home.

Davis was nervous for a completely different reason. His palms were sweating against the steering wheel. "No need to be. After what you did for Charlie and the way my kids go on about you, my parents already think you're terrific."

Traditionally, the entire Davis clan gathered at Mom and Dad's house on Christmas Eve for a light meal before heading to candlelight service at church. Christmas morning was reserved for the kids to open gifts and a return to Grandma's for dinner Christmas afternoon. This year, Davis no longer felt at loose ends. He had Lana, and being with her filled him with contentment.

"I don't want to embarrass you." Fingers spread, she jiggled her hands up and down in front of her body. "Is this outfit okay?"

He glanced at her, there in the passenger seat of his truck, full of gratitude that he'd had the good sense to see her value in time to salvage what neither had intended to start. He was also amused.

Did women always worry about their clothes being right? "You're perfect. Makes me want to drop off the kids and run away with you."

She laughed, flushing. "Maybe someday."

After tonight he'd know for sure if she really meant those words. Lana had choices she didn't know about. Davis wanted all her dreams to come true. He hoped he was one of them.

"Any word from Tess?" he asked, keeping his voice low.

Lana shook her head. "Not yet."

"Don't give up. It's Christmas."

He knew how badly she wanted to get her sister into rehab, but all their efforts so far were in vain. Tess had Lana's cell number. Davis prayed she'd someday make that call and ask for help.

"I'll never stop praying," Lana said. "If God can change my life, He can change hers, too."

As they pulled into his parents' driveway, Duncan, Dad's Great Dane, lumbered toward them, backlit by the red lights glowing around the roofline. Though they were dressed in Sunday best, the three kids tumbled out to roughhouse with the giant, friendly dog. The sharp air was spiced with wood smoke and, as soon as Mom opened the front door, all smiles, Davis smelled his favorite chicken gumbo.

Amidst introductions, kids whooping it up and the background of television blaring *It's a Wonderful Life,* they were sucked into the warmth of family. He knew Lana was nervous, especially around

Jenny, but she offered her help and disappeared into the kitchen with the other women. Mom would love her for chipping in.

In the living room, the men, including little Charlie, watched the familiar DVD. They'd watched it every Christmas Eve for as long as he could remember. Davis really wanted to talk to his dad in private, but the opportunity never presented itself. Tonight would be a surprise for him, as well.

One of the kids, Nathan he suspected, let Duncan in the house. The Great Dane went straight for the Christmas tree and snatched a candy cane before he could be wrestled back outside by the three guilty parties. Charlie laughed himself breathless which brought Jenny rushing into the living room.

After they'd stuffed themselves on gumbo and pecan pie, Davis glanced at his watch. Plenty of time before church. Lana sat at his side, the perfect spot and exactly where he'd planned for her to be. Where he always wanted her. But the choice was hers, starting now.

He waited for a pause in the conversation and when it finally came, he cleared his throat. A sudden fit of nerves danced in his belly. He reached for Lana's hand beneath the table and squeezed. She squeezed back.

"Everyone," he said, "I have something to say."

All eyes jerked to him and then to Lana. Speculative grins appeared on his parents' faces as they exchanged quick glances.

"Go ahead, son." Behind black-rimmed glasses, his dad's gaze was warm and encouraging. "If this is about you and Lana, I don't think any of us will be surprised."

His heart staccatoed. "It is. In a way." He shifted his chair to angle toward Lana. She'd turned a pretty shade of pink. Doing this in front of his family was harder than he'd expected. But absolutely right, too. He wanted Lana to know how proud he was of her. Here on Christmas Eve in front of the people he loved the most.

"Lana," he said and swallowed again. "I love you. My kids love you. We want you in our lives. You and Sydney. I never thought I'd feel this way about a woman again, but I do."

"I love you, too," she whispered, face red as Christmas but her blue eyes glowing with happiness. "I want—"

"Hear me out." He touched her lips with one finger, silencing her. "Before this goes any further, I have a Christmas present for you to open tonight."

Expression puzzled, she took the envelope from his hands and turned it over. "What is this?"

"It's one of your dreams. I want you to have it even if it means losing you."

"You won't—"

"I found Perry Grider."

"What?"

"Open the envelope, Lana."

He waited with a blood rush in his brain and his ears roaring while Lana read the letter.

"Someone wants to publish my song. For money." Astonishment quickly changed to excitement. "Is this legit? Is he for real? How did this happen?"

Though scared of losing her, Davis couldn't help the smile in his chest. He'd given her this and she was thrilled.

"Remember when you gave me the song? I told Joshua Kendle about it and asked if he knew anyone in the music business."

"I'd forgotten he once lived in Nashville."

"Yeah, well, he called around and this is the result. They not only want to buy this song, they want to see what else you have. They're interested in putting you under contract to write exclusively for GT Music."

"GT? No way. They're big-time."

He grinned, both proud and scared. "Merry Christmas."

"Is this for real?" She pressed the sheet of paper to her face and laughed in awe. "This can't be real."

He watched her delight and reveled in it, all the while wondering if he'd just given her a reason to leave Whisper Falls. His family began to talk all at once, excited for her.

Suddenly, a dimple cheeked boy pushed between them, expression stricken as he faced Lana. "Does this mean you're not gonna be my mom?"

The conversations quieted. Davis put a hand

on Nathan's shoulder, waiting for the answer, too. Slowly, Lana lowered the contract to her lap.

"Is that what you think?" she asked, incredulous. "That this would change the way I feel about you?"

"This is a game changer, Lana. You can move back to Nashville, write your songs, maybe even get another shot at a singing contract. This is your big chance."

"Yes, it *is* my big chance. To do the one thing I really want to do with my music…write songs. I don't want to live in Nashville. Been there, done that and have the scars to show. I don't want a singing contract. That life nearly destroyed me and Sydney. I want to write…but most of all, I want to be with you."

As if someone had turned on a vacuum and sucked out the anxiety, the tightness in Davis's chest eased.

"Positive?"

"More sure than I've ever been of anything."

"Nathan, son," he said as he gently moved his son to one side. "You'll have to excuse your old dad. I have a proposal to make."

Lana's hands flew to her mouth. "I'm going to pass out."

"Don't even think about it. I only want to do this once." Laughing at her a little and so thrilled, he thought *he* might pass out, Davis awkwardly maneuvered between the chairs and slipped to one knee in front of Lana.

"Lana Ross, I want to marry you and raise these kids together and if you want more, I'm good with that. I want to grow old with you, to share our lives and loves, to share your music. Will you give me the best Christmas gift a man could ever have? Will you be my wife?"

By the time he ended what he considered the longest speech of his life, Lana wept. No sound, but a waterfall of tears that touched him. His throat filled.

"Oh, yes." Her honeyed voice was thick with emotion as she whispered, "I would be honored."

They reached for each other, but before they connected, three small bodies barreled into the fray. The rest of the family was up, too, talking and pounding backs and grabbing hugs. Davis found Lana's gaze through the melee and winked.

"Meet you later," he said. "Under Nathan's mistletoe."

Through tears, she laughed and nodded.

And of course, they did.

* * * * *

Don't miss award-winning author
Linda Goodnight's next book in the
WHISPER FALLS *miniseries,*
on sale in 2014.
Look for it wherever
Love Inspired books are sold!

Dear Reader,

While the town of Whisper Falls is purely fiction, some of its elements are taken from existing Ozark communities. One of those is the train featured in this story as the "Christmas Express." Uncle Digger as engineer is, of course, a figment of my imagination, as is the Iron Horse, and other aspects of the depot. However, the Arkansas-Missouri Railroad is a true-to-life excursion train that served as my inspiration. The restored 1920's express zips sightseers from Van Buren's historic Old Frisco Station over the Arkansas River and through the gorgeous Boston Mountains. I hope you've enjoyed my fictional ride and the story of *Sugarplum Homecoming*.

I enjoy hearing from readers. You can sign up for my newsletter, read my blog, or send an email through my website: www.lindagoodnight.com. I'll look forward to hearing from you!

Merry Christmas,
Linda Goodnight

Questions For Discussion

1. Name and describe the hero and heroine in this story. Which was your favorite? Which could you best relate to? Were there other characters you particularly enjoyed? Which ones and why?

2. Lana Ross comes from a dysfunctional upbringing. Describe some of the things she went through as a child. How did these affect her teenage behavior? Do you think a negative environment is an excuse for bad behavior? Why or why not? What does scripture say about personal responsibility?

3. Lana went to Nashville to pursue a career in music. Have you ever followed a dream? What happened? What happened to Lana's dream?

4. Stage fright is a form of severe anxiety. What does Lana think caused her stage fright? Was she correct? Have you ever had something overwhelm you and you just couldn't get past it? What would help you overcome that fear?

5. How did Lana overcome her fear? What truth did she come to realize that helped set her free? Do think the change was realistic? Why or why not?

6. What sacrifice did Lana make and for whom? How did her sacrifice come back as blessings?

7. Why did Lana return to Whisper Falls instead of moving elsewhere? Do you think this was a good reason?

8. Lana's opinion of her self-worth was very low. How did Whisper Falls increase her feelings? Have you ever struggled with feelings of being "not good enough?" Are they possible to overcome? How?

9. Miss Evelyn asked Lana, "Don't you know who you are?" What did she mean? How should a relationship with Christ change our perception of self?

10. Davis's dreams have been shattered twice, but his reactions were different from Lana's. How did he handle the loss of his scholarship and the loss of his wife? Do you think family support made a difference?

11. Jenny, Davis's sister, harbors negative memories of Lana. Is it possible to hold a grudge for many years? What does the Bible teach about forgiveness? Is her son's illness an excuse for her behavior?

12. Lana thought she had to give up her music to follow God. Was this true? Why did she think so? How did her lifestyle affect her opinion? Does God expect us to give up who we are in order to have a relationship with Him?

13. Davis tells Lana that her music is a gift from God. Do you agree? The Bible says we all have gifts. What is yours? How are you using it?

14. Should a Christian's talents only be used in church-related fields? Or is it acceptable for a Christian to succeed in the secular world? Why or why not?

15. Lana lies to protect her niece. How did this affect her relationship with Davis? Is it ever right to lie? Would you lie to protect someone you love?

16. Near the end of the story, Lana and Davis come to terms with their problems and are free to start fresh. Have you ever been estranged from someone, or is there a relationship you would like to renew? What steps can you take to set things right?

17. Jenny quotes the scripture, "Don't cast your pearls before swine." Austin tells Davis, "Whom the Son has set free is free indeed."

What does each of these mean, and how do they relate to the story events? Which one best applies to Lana Ross?

LARGER-PRINT BOOKS!

GET 2 FREE LARGER-PRINT NOVELS PLUS 2 FREE MYSTERY GIFTS

Love Inspired®

Larger-print novels are now available...

LARGER-PRINT BOOKS!

GET 2 FREE LARGER-PRINT NOVELS PLUS 2 FREE MYSTERY GIFTS

Love Inspired®
SUSPENSE
RIVETING INSPIRATIONAL ROMANCE

Larger-print novels are now available...

YES! Please send me 2 FREE LARGER-PRINT Love Inspired® Suspense novels and my 2 FREE mystery gifts (gifts are worth about $10). After receiving them, if I don't wish to receive any more books, I can return the shipping statement marked "cancel." If I don't cancel, I will receive 4 brand-new novels every month and be billed just $5.24 per book in the U.S. or $5.74 per book in Canada. That's a savings of at least 23% off the cover price. It's quite a bargain! Shipping and handling is just 50¢ per book in the U.S. and 75¢ per book in Canada.* I understand that accepting the 2 free books and gifts places me under no obligation to buy anything. I can always return a shipment and cancel at any time. Even if I never buy another book, the two free books and gifts are mine to keep forever.

110/310 IDN F5CC

Name	(PLEASE PRINT)	
Address		Apt. #
City	State/Prov.	Zip/Postal Code

Signature (if under 18, a parent or guardian must sign)

Mail to the **Harlequin® Reader Service:**
IN U.S.A.: P.O. Box 1867, Buffalo, NY 14240-1867
IN CANADA: P.O. Box 609, Fort Erie, Ontario L2A 5X3

**Are you a current subscriber to Love Inspired Suspense books
and want to receive the larger-print edition?
Call 1-800-873-8635 or visit www.ReaderService.com.**

* Terms and prices subject to change without notice. Prices do not include applicable taxes. Sales tax applicable in N.Y. Canadian residents will be charged applicable taxes. Offer not valid in Quebec. This offer is limited to one order per household. Not valid for current subscribers to Love Inspired Suspense larger-print books. All orders subject to credit approval. Credit or debit balances in a customer's account(s) may be offset by any other outstanding balance owed by or to the customer. Please allow 4 to 6 weeks for delivery. Offer available while quantities last.

Your Privacy—The Harlequin® Reader Service is committed to protecting your privacy. Our Privacy Policy is available online at www.ReaderService.com or upon request from the Harlequin Reader Service.

We make a portion of our mailing list available to reputable third parties that offer products we believe may interest you. If you prefer that we not exchange your name with third parties, or if you wish to clarify or modify your communication preferences, please visit us at www.ReaderService.com/consumerschoice or write to us at Harlequin Reader Service Preference Service, P.O. Box 9062, Buffalo, NY 14269. Include your complete name and address.

LISLPDIR13R

ReaderService.com

Manage your account online!

- Review your order history
- Manage your payments
- Update your address

---

*We've designed
the Harlequin® Reader Service
website just for you.*

Enjoy all the features!

- Reader excerpts from any series
- Respond to mailings and special monthly offers
- Discover new series available to you
- Browse the Bonus Bucks catalog
- Share your feedback

Visit us at:
ReaderService.com

RS13